THE LETTER KILLS

*A romantic dramatic
thrilling crime comedy*

E. L. Kidwell

KIDWELL
PUBLISHING

Table of Contents

Chapter One

Spewing flames from its mouth and black smoke from its nostrils, the creature turned, rearing to catch the hero in its cutlass-like teeth. The knight's volley of poisoned arrows had failed to pierce the creature's armor, and instead only angered it beyond its already grumpy disposition. This beast was incapable of reason, and undeserving of mercy. Perhaps, if he could reach the head without being incinerated, then maybe he could blind the monstrous serpent. He could use another poisoned arrow and stab—but wait! The beast began roaring in human speech, "Joe! You see what I mean?!? You're not *listening*!"

Joseph's eyes rapidly blinked as his head shook in reflex. The thirty-two foot dragon vanished, and in its place was something much more devilish: his thirty-two year old wife. "What?!? Lily, I was listening! I was just distracted for a second."

Lillian screamed, "Agh! I hate you!"

Joseph loaded his bow, and let fly, "As if you're any better! You act like a damsel in distress to all your friends, but you act like a fire-breathing dragon toward me! You're the most hateful wench on the planet! I wouldn't be surprised if you …"

"If I *what*, Joe? Broke my vows?!? I would *never*, and you know why! *You* on the other hand …"

"Don't even try it, you witch! I've kept my vows, too, for the same reason, if for nothing else! That agreement is the only thing keeping you from taking everything I own."

"What do you mean, 'everything *you* own'? Or have you forgotten that I work, too! And I have as much invested as you have! You're such a total jerk!"

"Yeah, yeah! I've heard it all before. But *my* money was earned. Most of yours was just …"

"How dare you! I would rather have my father living than to have inherited his money! You hateful creep!!!"

Lillian's inner storm began pouring out of her. Memories of being "daddy's little princess" brought back the loss of her father six years ago as if had just happened today. And that heartache mingled with her husband's assaults was unbearable.

Joseph rolled his eyes in disgust, and walked out of the room. Lillian's pain mingled with rage began turning to resolve. She slowly fortified herself and quietly murmured, "God, I hate that man."

Their relationship hadn't always been like this. In fact, their childhood love and subsequent marriage had started off with the makings of greatness.

Joseph Brighton and Lillian Bonham had been friends long before they fell in love. Having been born only three weeks apart, they always seemed to be present together. Their families attended the same church, so Joseph and Lillian started life together in the nursery. This did not mean that they were romantically destined to be together. Nor did it mean they were unusually kind to one another. Little Joey sometimes stole little Lily's toys, and little Lily sometimes bit little Joey's arm. As they grew, Joey pulled her hair, and Lily kicked his leg. Joey would put a grasshopper on Lily's arm, and Lily would slap Joey's face. But with the resilience of kids, they couldn't hate for very long. And by the end of one day or the next, they managed to be friendly again—more or less.

By the age of nine, Lily's girlish view of Joey changed like the course of a butterfly. One moment she saw her prince and protector, the next she saw a toy: another one of her dolls to be dressed up and forced to drink tea.

Young Joey saw Lily almost the same as any of his other pals, except with a sort of handicap that made her more fragile: she was a *girl*.

He was a natural leader, and tended to view his friends as loyal subjects. But as he was a good king, he sincerely wanted the best for his citizens. He arranged the fun, he gave the orders, he expected them to obey, and they usually did.

Joey commanded, "Okay, we're going to play army. I'm the captain. Johnny, you be the sergeant."

Johnny saluted, "Yes sir!"

"Phillip, you can be the lieutenant." A salute.

"Moti, you setup the artillery … but don't fire them!"

Moti's face twisted like a pinwheel, "What's ar-til … ar-til-uh …"

"Artillery!" Joey interrupted. "It's the *big* guns."

Moti's joy stretched his grin like the band on his elastic undies, and he got to work moving unseen boxes of ammunition.

Lily, heretofore invisible to this army of little men, pleaded, "What can I be, Joey?"

Joey tried explaining, "We're going to *fight*, Lily. And you can't fight 'cuz you're a girl!"

In desperation, Lily replied, "But, I could do *something*! I know! I could be the nurse! I can take care of you when you get hurt!"

Joey deliberated about this like the captain he was, and agreed, "Okay, you can be the nurse. But stay away from the fighting."

"I will! And make sure you get hurt quick so I can make you better."

The battle lines were drawn, the allies advanced against the imagined enemy soldiers, and victory was inevitable. Despite the captain's orders, the nurse often ran onto the battlefield to give check-ups on the health of the soldiers, especially the captain. But no one really seemed to mind. They stuck out their tongues and said "Aah," and she looked into their mouths. She grabbed their wrists to check their pulse, and ensured them they were fit for duty. When the fun was done and the sun was setting, they all went home happy to have fought and won again.

One Sunday morning, as Joey was sitting in church, he found himself unusually interested in the preaching. Most Sundays, he would entertain himself by coloring in his Sunday School lesson book, or skimming through a book of illustrated Bible stories, or simply drawing. But today, Pastor Harkins had somehow captivated his attention. Joey's pen-in-hand sat limp on the drawing paper, and he was mesmerized by the message. He couldn't understand everything the preacher was saying. But what he did understand sounded something like this in his young mind:

"God *always* keeps His promises! You must *always* keep your promises! You must *never* break your word. Whatever you *say* you must *do*. If you break your *word*, you are breaking *yourself*!"

Through his youthful eyes and purity, Joey saw the world as purely monochromatic, and that was how he interpreted these phrases. Promises are *good*, and breaking promises is *bad*—everything was simply black-and-white. Thus he had his very first epiphany.

He knew what he needed to do: he must start a club. The very next day he gathered his friends, and announced his plan, "I'm going to start *The Promise Club!*"

Moti raised his hand out of habit, "What's a Promise Club?"

Joey continued, "It's *my* club. It's a club where everyone has to keep their word. Everything you say is a promise. So if you say you'll do something, then you have to do it."

Following Moti's example, Johnny raised his hand and spoke, "But what if you say something that you *can't* do, like jump ten feet?"

Stone-faced, Joey answered, "Then you're out of the club."

Phillip's hand raised, "What if you say you'll do something, but your parents won't let you?"

"Then you're out."

Lily's hand went up next, "What if you *want* to do something, so you *say* you'll do it, but then when you have to do it you don't want to anymore?"

Joey had expected everyone to simply sign up without any questions. Now frustrated, he raised his voice and shouted, "Then you're out!"

He looked around at the four lost puppies looking back at him—he hadn't meant to shout quite so loud. Proceeding with more reassurance, "I mean, you shouldn't *say* it if you're not gonna *do* it." And with the dignity of a king, he placed his right hand over his heart, and proceeded, "I'm the president. I now join The Promise Club. I will do what I say, and I will not say what I will not do. Are any of you going to join?"

Moti was moved to excitement by Joey's charisma, and threw his hand in the air, "I do! I do!"

Joey began leading him, "Okay, you must repeat The Pledge of the Promise Club."

"What's that?"

"The Pledge … you have to say the Pledge."

Moti placed his right hand on his heart, and began, "I pledge allegiance to the flag …"

"No!" Joey interrupted. "The *Promise Club* Pledge! It's different!"

"Oh! How's it go?"

Restraining his frustration, Joey calmly quoted, "'I now join The Promise Club. I will do what I say, and I will not say what I will not do.'"

After hard concentration, the pinwheel-face returned, and Moti asked, "Can you say that again?"

The others had also become interested. Joey habitually placed his right hand over his heart, and mimicking him, everyone tried to repeat his words verbatim. He managed to lead all four of them in saying the pledge, albeit in small pieces, and thus they were all successfully recruited into The Promise Club that day. As a matter of fact, no one quite said it right. But it was close enough for Joey to exclaim, "There! *We* are now the Promise Club!" He couldn't express it in words, but as he saw his friends there with him, he knew in his heart that this club was going to be the beginning of something that would guide them, and perhaps many others, faithfully into their glorious futures. But within four days, the only remaining members were himself and Lily.

The first day, Moti said flippantly that he wasn't scared to sneak into the neighbor's backyard with the big dog. But when pressured to do it he said, "I was only kidding." Joey reminded him about the club pledge, and that Moti *had* to do it.

Moti resisted, "I'm *not* doing it! That pledge is stupid!"

Joey cast his presidential judgment, "Then you're out of the club!"

Moti defiantly replied, "Good! Who wants to be in your stupid club anyway!"

Two days later, they were playing army again, and Phillip had to run home to use the restroom. He said, "I'll be right back," but he never returned.

The next day Joey told him, "You're out of the club."

Phillip explained, "But when I got home, my parents wouldn't let me go out again."

Joey justified, "Those are the rules."

Johnny got angry that Phillip got kicked out, so he quit.

Joey was hurt that his brand new club was already destroyed, so Lily tried comforting him. "I think your club is great, Joey! I'm still in! I *will* do what I say. See, I even remembered the pledge on my own!"

Joey replied inconsolably, "We can't have a club without *everyone*."

Then Lily's eyes widened with a clever thought. "Joey, you *said* you were starting The Promise Club. If you quit, then you are not doing what you *said*." Lily's words made perfect sense to him, and their encouragement was deeply received. Joey was still too young to fall in love, but in that moment, his view of Lily changed from that of a loyal subject to his royal equal.

"You're right! I *must* keep The Promise Club alive! You remember when we made buttons in Sunday School?

I'm going to make Promise Club buttons, and everyone will want to join again!"

As time progressed, The Promise Club never actually grew. Joey and Lily's buttons ended up stuck into posters hanging on their bedroom walls, then on their dressers, then in their sock drawers, and later in scrapbooks. But the club's effect on the two young people who had maintained their membership could not be overestimated. They began to grow into honest, principled, and diligent young adults. They succeeded in high school, and earned scholarships to college. They both chose Business Administration degrees, and even helped each other along from time to time.

By the time they were halfway finished with college, Joseph and Lillian's view of one another once again experienced a radical change. Lillian was no longer the girl who was merely a childhood friend. Joseph had become enchanted by her brown hair which wrapped around her ears, and hung about her neck like a charm. In her provocative eyes, he could perceive depths of joy throughout time. He admired the natural beauty in her smile, and the mystery in her smirk. He beheld her strength and her fragility, and he was in love.

To Lillian, Joseph was no longer just a boy. He was now a handsome and respectable young man, and the only man she desired to know. She saw in him her hopes of security and contentment.

During their last semester of college, they engaged to be married. After graduation they both secured jobs, and began planning their marriage in detail. One night, when Joseph went to Lillian's house to pick her up for dinner, he looked unusually pensive.

Lillian's father called out, "Lily, Joe's here to pick you up. You ready?"

Joseph sat down to wait, looking furtively at the floor. Lillian's father could tell that Joseph was thinking, and quietly said, "I'll be in the kitchen," as he left Joseph to his musings.

In a flash, Lillian appeared like a goddess, standing in the doorway across the room. Her presence shook Joseph's attention away from his thoughts like the last oasis in a world of sand.

"How do I look?" she asked coyly.

Joseph couldn't help replying excited, "You look outrageously gorgeous!"

Lillian's cheeks flushed for a moment, then she shouted around the corner, "Bye, Daddy! We're leaving!"

As the voice from the kitchen replied, Lillian mouthed the words as he spoke them, "Be back by eleven! Be good! Love you!"

She smiled smugly at Joseph, then shouted back to her father, "Love you, too!"

Joseph was the type of man who rarely made mistakes. His attention to detail seemed to be an inherent gift, one which was helping him rapidly excel in his work. And his time in college had taught him the importance of reading the fine print, crossing your T's, and dotting your I's. But at dinner that night, he was the town fool. As the waitress stood straining at her patience, Joseph was seemingly engrossed in the menu, and without looking up he asked, "Do you have ketchup for your fries?"

The waitress annoyingly glanced at the bottle of ketchup on the table, then at Lillian, then crackled with an embarrassed smile, "Uh, yessir, it's actually right here on the table!"

Not even noticing his error, he followed up with, "Do you have water?"

Coming to the rescue of the distressed waitress, Lillian interjected, "Why don't you give us a couple minutes?" A sigh of relief later, they were alone, and Lillian asked, "Joe, what's wrong? Are you alright?"

Joseph said, "What? Oh, yeah. I'm fine. I just …" Lillian was looking at him knowingly, and he felt compelled to confess. "Alright!" he continued. "I've just been wondering, what do you think about prenuptial agreements?"

Lillian cooly responded like a librarian quoting a dictionary, "Prenuptial agreement: a contract entered into prior to marriage, often for dispersal of property and assets in the event of adultery, divorce, or some other things I can't remember. Professor Grant wouldn't give me an 'A' for that definition, but …"

Joseph interrupted, "I'm serious, Lily. I've been thinking about our marriage. And I know this sounds childish, but I've been thinking about The Promise Club, too."

Lillian could see the difficulty Joseph was having, so she calmly replied, "Okay, I'm sorry for being silly. What's your point?"

He continued, "Well, I was wondering if you would be offended if we were to make a prenuptial agreement."

"Well, that would depend on whether the agreement was offensive."

"No, no … nothing like that. What I was thinking was that we could make a prenuptial agreement sort of like our old Promise Club."

With consideration, Lillian asked, "And what would the agreement actually state?"

"Essentially, it would say that if either of us were to break our vows—like filing for divorce, or by being unfaithful—then the other would get *everything*. In other words, it would make our vows really mean something. Instead of being just *words* that we might forget, they would actually be legal promises. They would be *real*."

"And what if we want to revise the prenup later in life?"

"Well, I suppose we could do that *if* we both agreed."

Lillian pondered this for a minute, and said, "Relax, Joe. I'm not offended. It's not a bad idea. *And* it means I can keep you all to myself forever and ever. And *that* part, I really like!"

Lawyers were called, documents were created, appointments were scheduled, names were signed, and fees were paid. The creed of The Promise Club was not actually written into their prenuptial agreement, but it was an unspoken understanding between them that keeping your word and honoring your vows were essentially one and the same.

Joseph and Lillian Brighton were lawfully married "until death do us part." Like the blur of a rollercoaster, their excitement in laying the foundations of an idyllic future together caused them to pass over certain consequences unnoticed.

Two years after their marriage, their dual-income lifestyle had placed them at the peak of middle-class society. And they each began to possess a secret selfish feeling toward their mutual affluence. He felt it was *his* success, and that she should be grateful to be enjoying such unearned security. She felt that without *her*, he would never have finished college, less yet been successful in business. And when she received her inheritance, she began feeling sure her financial contributions were more significant than his. In reality, they were both contributing almost equal amounts, both to their financial prosperity, and to their relational ruin.

Although most people physically mature by their early twenties, emotional maturity may come much later, if at all. For this twenty-seven year old couple, it was still quite absent. Had they been emotionally mature, they might have spent more time *helping* each other to bear life's burdens, and *sharing* in life's pleasures. But the perfection demanded by their club rules offered no mercy for human fact or frailty. What's worse, they seemed to relish the drumhead trials where they exposed and prosecuted the other's guilt. Instead of promoting virtuosity, their so-called "passion for promises" had created a degenerative and combative obsession in each of them.

One day, Joseph came home late from work, weary from the day's toil. He wanted nothing more than to sit down, talk about his day, take a shower, and try to relax before bedtime. But as awful as a Saturday alarm clock, Lillian asked, "Where's the milk?"

Joseph lamented to himself, "Darn it, I forgot the milk!"

With feline smugness, Lillian purred, "What what was that?"

Joseph growled, "I forgot!"

Batting him like a mouse in her paws, Lillian goaded, "But you *promised*!"

Joseph snorted as he headed back out the door, "Yes, I know! Don't worry, I'll go back out and get you your darned milk!" He was certain she was licking her paws as he slammed the door, and headed for the garage.

While driving to the store, Joseph tried to calm himself. He remembered back to when he was sixteen, and driving his first car. It was nicknamed *Old Faithful* because it spouted oil like its namesake. Joseph didn't think he could afford repairs, so he instead spent a small fortune on spare oil quarts which he carried in the trunk. He had to fill the oil more often than the gas, but he was just a teenager, and so he would often forget. Eventually, he ran the engine out of oil for several days when suddenly, bang! The car began shaking like a wet dog trying to dry itself, and then—pow! One last puff of smoke out the back, and the engine was dead. He knew that engines needed oil to last, but he had not done anything about it. When taken philosophically, this lesson might have prevented much of the coming disaster in his life. But he was an adolescent at the time, so we must grade on a curve. Even now, in his late twenties, as he was driving to the store, the engine of his marriage was several quarts low, and he had no intention of filling it up. He returned home with milk, and not another word passed between he and his wife for several days.

After four more years of high salaries, profitable investments, and an inheritance, Joseph and Lillian jointly owned nearly a million dollars worth of assets, as well as a quarter-million dollars in cash, spread across a few different accounts. But despite their wealth, their relationship was almost completely destroyed. The innocent love they had originally enjoyed had gone *pow!* long ago, and they needed a total overhaul.

One Saturday, Joseph was playing at his computer when he received a message. He asked, "Lily, did you pay our mobile bill?"

Lily replied uncertainly, "I think so … didn't I?"

Joseph gloated, "I just received a message that it's now *late*. You *said* you would take care of it a week ago, but you *didn't*!"

Embarrassed and angry, she griped back, "I must've *forgot*! I'll pay it online right now! Sheesh!"

Joseph secretly grinned at her failure, but offered no consolation. The fantasy war game on his computer supplied his modus operandi: engage the enemy, us versus them, kill or be killed, attack! Marital life was martial life. Within five minutes, Lillian had taken care of the overdue bill, but the anger she felt would not so soon subside.

In their marriage, promise-keeping and truth-telling had been distorted into mercilessness and self-righteousness. Once-deep love was turned to deeper hatred. Once-noble virtues had become wicked vices. Irony often sickens those who create it, and the Brighton couple was showing symptoms of terminal illness.

Another year of this warfare brought them to their present hostility, where the festering hatred in Joseph's heart has led him to view Lillian as an unredeemable dragon; and Lillian hates Joseph with a perfection greater than any love for which she married him.

Chapter Two

Moti had not been fortunate. To Life, he was a scavenging sewer rat, detested when hungry, and resented for every morsel he stole—even if it had been discarded. Other than struggling to build a bigger nest, sniffing for finer food, and searching for a nice hole, Moti had done nothing to earn such disdain. As far as rats go, he was a good one. But it's unkind to paint this man with the palette of Life's judgment, for only someone as cruel as Life itself would picture this poor creature as a rat. Life is unfair, and Moti was, after all, a man.

In his own mind, Moti was a Renaissance Man. He had started working young, and acquired a plethora of skills over 15 years of trying to find his way. He would boast, "I've been a professional chef, an interior designer, a relocation specialist, an automotive engineer, and a flooring expert." Others saw those jobs merely as a burger-flipper, a painter, a mover, an oil-change mechanic, and a carpet cleaner. But, like so many people, Moti preferred his house to have all the mirrors facing the wall.

Two years ago, Moti had elevated himself to being an "entrepreneur," and he relished the sound of that. He had managed to buy his own carpet cleaning machine, an old van, and some thermographic business cards. To his credit, he was a conscientious carpet cleaner. He relied on certain websites for his jobs, so maintaining a good reputation was of vital importance to him. He would often check his online profile for customer ratings and reviews, and worked hard both to please and appease. When work was slow, he would spend the time researching the latest cleaning chemicals, and interacting with suppliers. Sometimes he would secretly indulge the conceit that he could handle the toughest cleaning job, or the most abrasive customer. But that was a small flaw in his otherwise good-natured disposition.

Sunday afternoon, Moti was at his computer bidding on cleaning jobs that he hoped to win. It had been a slow week, and he knew if he didn't get some jobs lined up immediately, he would have to face Missus McGraw. She was a ruthless landlady who only ever wore black slacks, a white shirt, and a black jacket. Her eyes seemed smaller than natural due to her thick-lensed glasses which were supported by thick black frames. Moti secretly called her "McCaw!" and envisioned her as a pesky pied crow, always making noise when you want it quiet. It was not the first time he struggled to make rent, and he cringed at the idea of having to look into McCaw's beady little bird eyes, and explain that he would be late. Suddenly, bing! His phone alerted him, "Your bid was accepted!" Moti sighed and shouted a victorious "yes!" with a fist pump. It was the job at Ross Boyd Jewelers, and it was scheduled first thing tomorrow.

In the morning, Moti was already waiting in the parking lot when a white-haired man walked to the front doors of the jewelry store, and began opening up. He unbarred and unchained the roll-up security door, pushing it upward and out of sight, then unlocked the previously hidden double-door entrance. Concealed by the noise, Moti had walked up behind his back, and greeted him with perky morning cheer, "Good morning, Sir!"

The man appeared to have touched an electric fence! He visibly jumped, dropped his keys, and glared back at Moti with sparks of electricity still flashing in his eyes. He snarled his disgust, and disappeared inside the unlit building. Moti had bent down to get the keys the man had dropped, and when he stood up the man was gone, leaving Moti standing with his hand extended like a Salvation Army Santa. Seconds later, the inside lights flickered their resistance to the morning before staying on, and the grumpy man reappeared at a distance inside. Throwing the door open, he glared at Moti.

"You dropped your keys," Moti uncomfortably observed, extending the keys like a peace offering.

"Give me those!" griped the man, snatching the keys from Moti's fingers. "Who are you, and what are you doing sneaking up on me?"

Gesturing to his van with the words "Carpet Cleaning" boldly displayed, Moti offered a business card and answered, "I'm the flooring expert from Moti's Carpet Cleaning. You accepted our bid yesterday, and we're here prompt and early to make you the happiest customer ..."

Looking at the card and ignoring most of what Moti was saying, the man interrupted, "Oh, yeah, the carpet. I had tried to forget. Well, go ahead and get started. You need to be finished before nine-thirty because we open at ten."

Unaffected by the man's disposition, Moti responded with a chipper smile, "Right away, sir! And what is your name, sir?"

"Ross Boyd."

"Oh! Mister Boyd! I didn't expect to meet *you* here today. It is a pleasure to meet you, and I want to assure you that our service ..."

"It must be *perfect*."

"Yessir. We do our absolute best, and may I say ..."

Ross had turned to go inside, but stopped with his back to Moti, and raised his voice slightly to interrupt, "No, you may not 'say.' Just get the carpet cleaned so that you are gone before any customers arrive."

Moti rightly took offense at the snobbery of this man, and could not stop himself from mouthing the words, "What the...?!?"

Ross remained standing there, staring at the storefront windows. His disposition changed, and he explained, "On Saturday, that duchess brought her stupid cat into my store." Ross talked to the reflection of the horizon as he recounted the grim tale in melancholy tones. "She arranged an appointment—all the way from Europe—to order a custom four carat diamond ring. When I saw her approaching from outside …" The grumpy man now seemed to be transported into a dream. His features softened, and his eyes looked further into the distance, adrift in space. He spoke like a heartbroken husband, remembering the beloved wife whom he knew to be alive somewhere, but from which he had been forever separated by a tragic shipwreck. "She was … beautiful. She was sublime in her manner, and walked with royal grace. Every step seemed deliberate. And she was captivating. I thought to myself, 'She floats like an angel!' And when she approached the door, my humble hovel seemed unworthy to receive such dignity." Then the nostalgia drained from his expression, and his scowl returned as he exclaimed, "But she stank!!! Dear God, she must've lived in a castle of cats! The revulsion of my olfactories nearly prevented me from taking her money. What's worse is she brought one of the smelly vermin with her—into my store! And then her fricking feline soiled my showroom carpet!!!"

As soon as Moti heard these words, he looked anxious, and started thinking about his chemicals. He knew that if the smell had already seeped into the padding under the carpet, he would not be able to completely remove it. His first instinct was to level with Ross, and suggest that the carpet be replaced.

"Mister Boyd, I think you should know that …"

Ross was irritated, and assumed Moti was rambling on with more self-praise and service industry clichés.

"Just get it done!" he barked, and stormed back inside.

Moti was getting angry. He had done his best to maintain an appearance of professionalism and courtesy, but this man was obnoxious. Moti imagined himself stomping inside, putting his finger in Ross's chest, and saying, "You may know royalty, but I know carpets! You ain't never getting that smell out, and I ain't letting you tell me nothing!" But as he was preaching the carpet gospel, Ross transformed into a bird and began squawking, "Caw! Caw! Missus McCaw!" The bird started flapping, diving and clawing at his head, and Moti jumped awake. He was still standing outside, struck with the unpleasant reality of his situation. He had to pay rent, so he had to do something to try and make some money. "Well," he thought as he encouraged himself, "I am an *entrepreneur* and an expert in my field. I can do this!"

Moti cleaned the carpet, combing the problem area with his machine like Rapunzel searching for a buried knot of hair. He increased the amount of detergent, and went the extra mile trying to eradicate the stink. The building had been closed up for more than a day, pickling in those caustic fumes. So Moti worked his magic, and conjured a potion of industrial strength air freshener. He hoped that the miasma could be dispelled before his craft expired. But he knew all too well that the bewitchments of felines are not easily exorcised.

After packing his equipment back in the van, Moti returned to the showroom, and called out to the back area of the shop where Ross had disappeared, "I'm all done, Mister Boyd!"

Ross appeared, and sniffed the air, "Definitely smells better, but I think I can still smell some *cat*."

Moti hurriedly explained, "That's just temporary, sir, because the building was closed up yesterday. Once it airs out, it should be fine. However, if—on the off chance and slightest possibility—the smell comes back, you may need to replace the carpet and padding … in the worst case, that is." Moti was certain the smell *would* come back, and that Ross *must* replace the carpet. But right now, he just wanted to get paid, so he quickly changed the subject to what was on his mind. "In a few minutes," Moti explained, "you'll receive an electronic invoice in your email. Follow the instructions, and you can pay your bill online in less than five minutes—it's very simple!" Moti needed this payment quickly, and his attempts to sound cheery revealed this more than they concealed it.

Back in his van, Moti was feeling optimistic now that his rent would be paid, and so he decided to treat himself to a luxurious brunch before returning home. He stopped by his favorite roadside stand, and enjoyed a meal that, as Moti often said, "would make King Solomon jealous": a giant burrito filled with *huevos, frijoles, arroz,* and *papas con chorizo,* all washed down with *horchata.*

Afterwards, he moseyed his way back home, and logged in to his favorite website to check on new bid opportunities, and review customer feedback. Reading the screen, Moti's face went pale, and he actually shouted to himself, "Oh, no! This ain't happening!!!" To his horror, there was a brand new and scathing review from none other than Ross Boyd Jewelers! Moti's eyes blinked as if they were being poked by toothpicks as he continued reading. Mister Boyd's words were concise if not specific. Moti uttered the most shocking words out loud as he read, "Lack of etiquette?!? Offensive?!? Disgusted?!?" But the last two words hurt Moti the most, and he jumped out of his seat as he shouted, "Won't pay?!?" A flood of obscenities filled his apartment. Moti ran out to his van, and set a course for Ross Boyd Jewelers. He didn't think about *why* he was going there—whether to beg for payment or to inflict bodily harm. But in the heat of his anger, he instinctively drove on, feeling the need to face Ross Boyd personally.

Chapter Three

When angry, human beings often lose emotional perspective. Imagine standing on a straight stretch of railroad track, and looking off in the distance. The tracks always appear foreshortened, as if they are getting narrower the farther off you look. In reality, they are always 1,435 millimeters apart, even if your perspective makes them appear to touch in the distance. Although our eyes might consider perspective to seem dishonest, it is the only way we are able to tell if that train in the distance is coming or going, whether a danger is far or near. Thus, visual perspective regularly protects us. Emotional perspective is much the same. It can help us to distance our present feelings from past hurt, and can even offer hope and safety for our future. It can enable us, when looking down those tracks in our memory, to recognize any approaching train wrecks in the present. Thus, maintaining emotional perspective can qualify as one of the great virtues a human being can practice. But anger has a way of quickly destroying our emotional perspective, and makes everything feel like *now*. The tracks of time become orthographic, and we no longer consider any trains in the distance, whether past or future. And thus, we crash.

Moti had certainly lost his perspective. He arrived at the store like a warhorse storming the front lines. He parked his van across two parking spots, jumped out, and began marching toward the store entrance. He burst through the double-doors, and with a maniacal quiver in his voice shouted, "Where's Ross?!?" The electric sizzle in his voice disrupted this environment of restraint and dignity like a lightning bolt in a petting zoo. The middle-aged bunny-woman working behind the counter jumped for an instant, and now seemed to be frozen. She had been helping a young couple pick out their wedding jewelry, and their concentration on their rings numbed them slightly to this surprise. They slowly turned, like a disinterested pair of goats chewing on their cud, to see the culprit. The worker scratched off her discomposure, and spoke with an air of aristocracy, "I'm sorry, sir. I was busy helping these customers. If you'll please wait a moment, I'll be …"

Moti's lightning struck again, "Where's Ross?!?"

The woman glared in disgust at Moti's disregard for dignity, and while dialing on her intercom phone she blurted, "Oh, very well! Mister Boyd, there's a man here to see you. No, I don't believe he's a customer." With a forced smile she replaced the handset and said, "He'll be right out. Now if you don't mind, these people were here before you." She apologized to her clients, and resumed her work.

Ross appeared from the back, revolted at the sight of this carpet cleaning rat. Like a miser to a beggar, Ross asked, "What do you want?"

Moti, trying to regain some semblance of *entrepreneur*, replied with nervous agitation, "I would like … I wanted to … in your review … "

Ross's words blew like November's gales, "If you've read my review, then there's nothing to discuss," and he turned to walk away.

Overcome with anger and desperation, Moti began to shout, "I need that money! I used my chemicals—lots of them! And they're expensive! I have to pay rent! I did my best!" and a dozen more pleadings and protests that fell on Ross's deaf ears.

Ross calmly reached under the counter and covertly pressed a hidden emergency button. Then he turned back, feigning attention to Moti's ramblings for several minutes, so as to detain him until the police arrived.

Wee-ooo-wee-ooo-wee-ooo! Two police cars, with lights flashing, quickly pulled up in front of the store. Moti turned to see what was going on outside, and turned back to see Ross's face with an arrogant smirk. Moti pleaded, "You called the cops? Why'd you call the cops?!?"

Ross, looking as if laser beams were coming out of his eyes, retorted almost in a whisper, "Kid, you're not the first rat I've put my cat on."

The moment the police entered, Moti lost both his perspective and his temper. He began shouting profanities that questioned Ross's genetic structure. He cursed Ross's parentage, and alleged lawless occupations of three generations of his mothers. And then insults turned to threats, "You won't get away with this, you S.O.B.! I'll kill you! I'll kill you!!!"

An officer had entered the building, and repeatedly asked Moti to calm down and lower his voice. But nothing could stop Moti's screaming until he heard a ratcheting sound—brrtrtr-click! Moti's arms had been pulled behind him, and bound in handcuffs.

Officer Jacobs led Moti outside, and locked him in the back of his police car. Jacobs said he was going inside to collect witness statements, and that he would return in ten-to-fifteen minutes. "Don't go anywhere," he joked as he shut the door. But within three minutes, he was exiting the store, and opened the car saying, "You're free to go, Mister Martinez, on one condition. Mister Boyd is willing to drop any charges *if* you leave this property right now and do not return."

Being handcuffed and deprived of liberty for a few minutes had forced Moti into momentarily controlling his temper, and regaining his perspective. He had no disrespect for the law nor its officers, even if, in his opinion, they were currently protecting the *bad* guy. Moti replied sheepishly, "But what about my rent? What about my record?"

Jacobs reassured him, "There will still be a police report on file, but nothing will go on your criminal record. And I'm afraid I can't help you with your rent, but at least you'll be free to work." Then he looked at Moti with an encouraging grin and said, "Now go on home, and try not to get into any more trouble."

Although Moti was relieved at being let off, he was still furious at Ross, and worried about McCaw. His van drove out of the parking lot like a beaten dog. He felt like everyone on the street was looking at him; every casual glance from the car next door was accusing him, mocking him, taunting him. He felt like they all knew that he had just been arrested, that he had been ripped off, that he was a fool, that he was—Moti spoke the words to himself—"a Loser." He was stopped at a red light, and his head hung in despair. Beep, beep, beeeep! The light had turned green. Moti felt like a man stranded on the moon with limited time before his air would run out. He began looking for a place to breathe.

Down the street, Moti spotted a sign: *Hemlock Tavern*. If he had read Shakespeare or had any knowledge of Hamlet's unfortunate father, he might of hesitated. But Moti figured a *hemlock* was something like a zipper, and therefore, nothing to fear. The bar had just opened, but already there seemed to be a small crowd of men who must've slept there. The room was dark and musty, but the stains on some of the men's tattered white teeshirts were easy to see. Ironically, there was no smoke in the air, which Moti liked. He figured that if this bar obeyed the no-smoking law, it must be a good establishment.

Moti parked himself on a stool, and tried swimming in a bottomless bottle. Some might say he was, "drowning his sorrows," but that is like trying to drown a fish. In fact, he was drowning himself, and his sorrows would still be there whether or not he survived. He was not a regular drinker, and didn't even like alcohol. His biological father had died from alcohol poisoning when he was two years old, and Moti had always feared liquor because of it. But the day had thrown him into the deep end of the bottle, and Moti was sinking.

Moti considered himself to be a heavy drinker, but not of alcohol. His body had been conditioned to handle large quantities of sweet teas and sodas, as was evidenced by the dozens of empty jumbo cups littering the floorboards on the passenger side of his van. But at this bar, he was a drowning man, scuttling what was left of his self-esteem. Like the calls of a crane, he let the world know his complaints against it. With false starts and short stops, he drunkenly lamented, "Darn you, Mister Ross Boyd Jewelers! You're gonna pay … for ripping me off! I don't know how … or who—why … I meant, I mean … why … I meant to say *why*—but *you* know why! 'Cuz you're a *liar*! And that means you *lie*! And that's not all …"

Three stools away sat a muscle-bound and tattooed terror of a young man. His shirt seemed to be shrink-wrapped around every striated muscle of his lean body. And if meanness goes with leanness, this must've been Leroy Brown's modern protégé. He had a single shot of whiskey in his hand, and although he was looking straight ahead, he seemed to be observing everyone in the room. For the past few minutes, Moti had been unaware of anyone else, including this frightful figure nearby. Then the creature turned, and called out to Moti, "Hey! Sss-up? What's your name?"

"My name? My name is …" Moti had to think. "I know I knew my name a minute ago. Oh, yeah … I remember it … now, that is … I remember now." And Moti laughed with such drunken sincerity that even Mister Muscles chuckled.

Muscles continued, "So, are you going to tell me what it is?"

"What is what … what is?" Moti stammered.

"You're name," he laughed.

"Oh! My name's Moti! Like, 'Mooooooh-teeeeee'!" Moti shouted back as if he thought Muscles was Chinese.

Muscles laughed out loud, and asked, "Moti, huh? How'd you get a name like 'Moti'?"

Moti, in his drunken bliss and ignorance, proceeded to tell his life story.

"When I was a baby, I was born. And I was born a baby, so my daddy named me after all his mommies and daddies before him. And he named me Martin Martinez Ochoa Escondido the Third!" Moti held his glass in the air and said his own name as if it were the name of an honored king. "Now, no sooner did my daddy give me that name … he died." Moti began to cry. He had no memories of his father, but the sadness of those words under the influence of booze just made him start crying. Sniffling away the sadness he continued, "But I was a lucky kid, and my mama was a beautiful woman. So a couple years later she met and married my dad—well, my *stepdad* … but he was better to me than some kids' *real* dads. I told you, I was lucky! Anyway, when I was about four, Dad started calling me Moe—because of my initials, M-M-O-E. You understand? It was his way of making me feel special. Well, my mama was from Mexico, and she was still learning English when I was young. And when she was upset she would call me, 'Manuel Martinez Ochoa Escondido Three!' But because of her Spanish accent, the word *three* always ended up sounding like *tea*, like a cup of *tea*. Dad thought that was funny, so he started calling me Moe-Tea. So by the time I started school, I was Moti forever. And since I told you my name, now you gotta tell me yours."

Muscles snickered, "Yo! I'm G."

Moti looked cross-eyed at him, and said, "Only *one* initial?!?"

G got up, came over, and sat down in the stool right next to Moti. He leaned in, and talked in hushed tones, which Moti's suggestive state imitated. G explained, "I heard you complaining … some guy ripped you off, right? I might be able to help."

Over the next hour, G proceeded to extract Moti's story in detail, and to get Moti so enraged he was ready to drive back to Ross Boyd Jewelers and commit first-degree murder then and there. Once Moti was so enraged, G played the sympathetic friend who suggested that, if Moti didn't want to go to jail, he could *hire* someone to do the deed—a hitman. Moti's drunken mind, so open to suggestion, could only see black and white. Jail, black. Hitman, white. Yes, of course! It was a great idea!

G asked, "You got any assets?"

Moti was too disgraced to admit the truth, so he looked at G with all the focus his drunken eyes could muster, and asserted, "I'll have you know, sir, I'm an *entrepreneur*! I was actually *slumming* when I agreed to work at Boyd's place."

G pretended to be impressed, and began to explain the procedures for a meeting with his contact. Moti would get inside the white S.U.V. parked behind the building. Once inside, he would be blindfolded until he was in the meeting room with the agent. When his meeting was concluded, he would again be blindfolded while in the meeting room, and driven back to the Hemlock Tavern. And anything that could possibly have GPS was not allowed. Moti agreed, and left his phone in his van before climbing into the S.U.V. for his blindfolded journey. In his inebriated state, the darkness of the blindfold and the comfort of the ride caused him to doze off. He couldn't tell if he had been driving one minute or one hour when the sudden stop of the vehicle woke him up. Although G looked like a bulldog, he guided Moti like a seeing-eye dog. Moti's mind was still confused, but he felt like he was inside the garage of a house. Certain sounds faintly echoed off the interior walls: the car door closing, a cough, a foot scuffing the ground. They stopped, and Moti heard soft beeps as G tapped some keys on a digital lock. Then a door opened. After Moti was guided through, he heard the servos of the digital lock fasten the door behind him —bzzzzzzzt click! Then Moti felt like a rat in a cheese-maze: pulled forward, turned right, forward again, right again, forward, left, stop, turn, forward, stop. G led Moti into a small room, sat him down in a chair, and without a word, walked out of the room. All was silence. Moti was certain he was alone, and started to reach for the blindfold. Immediately, a deep voice with the richness of a Bible narrator sounded out of the emptiness in front of him. And the contradiction of soothing tone and threatening calmness filled Moti with revulsion. It said, "Please don't touch that. I'll remove it when I'm ready."

There is nothing so terrifying as intelligent evil. Moti involuntarily jumped in his chair as if it had been momentarily connected to an electrical outlet. Still blindfolded and silly, he resituated himself as upright as possible, and spoke in a nervous voice that worked too hard to command respect, "Yes! Of course. No problem. I apologize. I didn't see you there." Moti heard no sound in the room, but the man was suddenly behind him, removing the blindfold.

Up until now, Moti had imagined that he was in film noir: meeting in a dingy room in a weary industrial building, and that the hitman would be wearing a tailored pinstriped suit and fedora. Two things quickly surprised him. First, he was inside a brightly lit home office in what looked like a newly constructed home. Second, the man before him was wearing a teeshirt, shorts, and sneakers, and looked like he had just returned from a jog. But despite his leisurely clothing, his physique was lean and muscular, and his visage seemed to have been carved from lava rock. Moti's head was still spinning, and he unthinkingly asked, "Who are you?"

"You can call me Kite."

Moti looked confused, "Like 'flying a *kite*'?"

Kite huffed, "Like the *bird* … the bird of *prey*!"

"Oh, sorry. I never heard of it."

"Well, Mister Moti, I have heard of you. I have heard that you did a job for Mister Ross Boyd, a jeweler. I have heard how he made a fool of you and ripped you off. I have heard that you yelled at him in front of his employee and a young couple. I have heard that you were arrested, commanded to leave the property, and let off with a warning."

Moti could not hide his bewilderment, and asked Kite as well as himself, "How'd you know all that?"

"Like you, Mister Moti, I'm a businessman. And I research my craft."

"But I never told G 'bout the couple."

"Yes, I suppose that's true. But now I know it, and because I know it you should know that I am a professional. I have my suppliers, just like you have yours. You buy carpet detergent, I buy information." Kite paused like a king delivering a speech who wanted to ensure that his subjects understood the gravity of his words. Then continuing, "So, to brass tacks. I understand you. You understand me. We need to discuss timing and payment, and you can go on your way." Kite proceeded to enumerate his terms and conditions like a realtor at escrow. "I recommend that you immediately distance yourself from The Package. Tomorrow you must apologize, and make sure there are witnesses."

"Apologize! *He's* the one that ripped off *me*, remember?!?"

"Yes, and if anything happens to him now, *you* will be the chief suspect. Understand?"

Moti's brow crinkled in thought, but he was distracted by an approaching headache.

Kite continued, "So, tomorrow you will call The Package. Be sure to tell whoever answers that you are calling to apologize. And also send it in writing: both email and postal mail. I will monitor The Package for a while, and you can monitor the news. Payment terms are half up front, and half when The Package is delivered."

Moti had been holding his throbbing head in his hands, but at the mention of payment, he looked up. He had been so angry and drunk when he came, he had overlooked his obvious problem: lacking money for rent meant lacking money for anything. Moti squeaked, "How much is 'half up front'?"

"Ten thousand dollars, fifty percent of twenty. And don't worry about the feds. I have setup several charities where large donations are commonplace."

"But I don't have that kind of money!"

"Don't you have any assets? A house? A car? A fleet of vans? Business equipment? Anything?!?"

"Just my one van, my carpet machine, and my computer ... nothing near twenty grand!"

Kite's jaw tensed as if he was chewing old gum. He picked up his phone and seemed to be sending a message. Thirty seconds later, the door behind Moti opened, and G entered. Kite stared fiercely at G, but said calmly, "Mister Moti is *insolvent*. But you should have known that already."

Like an ox driven by a plowman, G was ordinarily subdued before Kite. To view them physically, a Las Vegas man would always bet on G in a hand-to-hand struggle. But Kite, with a military disposition and discipline, ordered his thugs like soldiers, and they obeyed.

In this moment, G was confused by the reprimand and exclaimed, "He said he was an 'entrepreneur'!"

Kite never blinked as he continued to stare with eyes of fire, and G acquiesced, "Sorry, Kite. My bad. Won't happen again."

Kite sneered in disgust, and replaced the blindfold as if trying to save his own eyes from having to see Moti's face again. The light had been pounding Moti's head for several minutes, so he was only too happy to have the blindfold back. G led him out of the room, through the house, and back to the vehicle.

As they drove away, Kite remained in his office glancing at a police report from Moti's arrest which he had acquired from his "supplier." A sinister grin briefly appeared, and Kite began to talk to himself. "On second thought, this is a *perfect* opportunity. One to take the bullet, and one to take the blame."

Chapter Four

Tuesday morning at the office, Alan quickly peeked his head around Joseph's office door, and shouted in a whisper, "We're getting subs. You wanna go?"

Joseph jumped in his seat. He had been trying to review a spreadsheet from one of his subordinate managers, and had become hypnotized by the numbers. The characters on the screen seemed to be ASCII-art of Lillian with an angry scowl. She was always scolding, complaining, and screaming. And even now, miles away in the refuge of his private office at work, she had managed to intrude and disquiet his thoughts. Trying to hide his surprise, he looked at Alan who wasn't trying at all to hide his smirk, and said, "Sure. I could use a break."

"Obviously!" Alan chuckled as his head floated out of the doorway.

At the sub shop, Joseph shared a table with four other guys: Charlie the Accounting Manager, Matt a Junior Accountant, Ralph a Business Process Analyst, and Alan the Marketing Manager. Although Joseph was the Director of Finance and had a great deal of prestige on the Organizational Chart, he was still sociable with people regardless of their work title. Some coworkers thought that it was this trait more than any other that had earned him such a respectable position. Others thought that it was his attention to details. Whatever the cause for his promotion, everyone agreed that he deserved it, if for no other reason, on the grounds of shear likability.

Speaking through his sub, Alan asked, "So what'd you guys do this weekend?"

Joseph silently ate.

Charlie answered, "I took my wife out to a quiet dinner and a movie. To be honest, I thought it was all boring as heck, but that's a small price for me to pay since she seemed to like it."

Matt interjected while trying to chew, "Oh, yeah! I took my wife out, too."

Alan rescued him with a laugh, "Don't choke yourself, Matt! Where'd you take her?"

Matt swallowed and continued, "I took her on a date downtown, to see that monster truck rally."

Like Mount Vesuvius, the table erupted into laughter, and most of the men ended up swallowing whole bites and gulping their drinks to catch their breath.

Charlie recovered first, "You took your wife to a truck rally as a *date*?!?"

Matt defended himself, "Well, she seemed to like it, especially the mud wrestling."

Like a double eruption from a supervolcano, their lava-laughter again flooded the small restaurant as all other patrons stopped to watch.

Charlie responded good-naturedly, "You might be a redneck *if*—!"

Alan began confessing, "Well, that's why I'm not married. Here's Charlie's wife who likes dinner-and-a-movie, and Matt's likes mud wrestling. And only God knows if they'll still like the same thing next week. Am I right?"

Joseph laughed, but was uncomfortable with today's wife topic, and nervously picked certain pieces of wilted lettuce from his sub.

Glancing away from Joseph, Alan asked, "What about you, Ralph? What's your wife's favorite date?"

Ralph was still chuckling at Matt, but as he began to think about the question, his attention seemed to drift far away as he spoke, "I'm not sure. We've already been married over three years, but sometimes I feel like I don't really know her at all. I ask her, 'What would you like to do?' and she answers, 'Whatever *you* want to do.' And it's like, I just want to do something special for *her*, but she doesn't seem to want to tell me what it is that she *wants*. So I always feel like I'm guessing, and that she's never really happy."

All the guys had tensed up at his honesty except for Charlie, who was sitting there grinning. Charlie was the oldest and most experienced in matters of marriage, and everyone thought that he should be the one to answer. "What your wife *wants*," he said, "is to make *you* happy, you big dummy! She simply wants to be with you when you are enjoying yourself, and to share in those joyful moments. You're analyzing her too much, Ralph."

Alan looked back to Joseph, who seemed to be arguing with himself, and asked, "What about your wife, Joe? What does she like?"

Before Joseph could stop his mouth from speaking, the words blurted out, "To make me miserable!"

Across town, Lillian had just returned to her desk to eat lunch.

For several years, she had been the office manager for a medium-sized electronics manufacturer. In the eyes of the board of directors, she possessed two valuable assets. First, her dedication was unparalleled, which meant several aspects of their market growth were directly traceable to her efforts. Second, she was perhaps the best looking woman in the company. It would have been offensive—if not illegal—to admit such a base notion, and so they didn't. But in an environment where most of the employees were soldering circuit boards on an assembly line, Lillian was one of the few women on-site whose beauty wasn't concealed by safety goggles and a bouffant cap. The Board of Directors believed that, if not for her charm, they might not have secured at least two of their more lucrative contracts. But these things could never be spoken in the workplace.

Just as Lillian took a bite of her salad, Joanna, one of the line supervisors, walked in. Over the past year, Lillian had become more than just Joanna's boss. They had become good friends. Lillian looked up embarrassed, and accidentally dropped salad dressing on her chin. Apologetically, Joanna began, "I'm sorry … I didn't mean …"

"No problem," Lillian mumbled through her lettuce. "What'cha need?"

"Actually, I figured you'd be eating at your desk, and wanted to see if I could join you."

"Yes, of course! Come in! Have a seat!" Lillian was only too happy to have some company.

Joanna opened up her plastic container, and the savory aroma of leftover spaghetti filled the room.

"That smells delicious!" Lillian said, deeply breathing through her nose.

"My husband made it Friday night … totally surprised me! He arranged this 'romantic getaway' without even having to leave the house. He had already taken the kids to stay with my mom, decorated the table, cooked spaghetti, and …"

Lillian's jealousy was a complex mixture of happiness for Joanna, and anger toward her own husband. And the feelings provoked by these words were stronger than she thought she could control. Trying to suppress her welling emotions, she interrupted, "Any occasion? Anniversary?"

"That's just what surprised me," Joanna continued joyfully, "there was no occasion! We talked and laughed over dinner, and well … let's just say we slept until noon on Saturday." Joanna coyly bit her lip, and smiled.

Lillian had stopped eating, and was listening wistfully. The internal pressure had quickly built up, and like the bursting of a dam, the anger and pain poured forth in bawling tears. Joanna was momentarily in shock, then courteously stepped up and closed the door to the office. Speaking sympathetically, "I'm so sorry, Lily. I honestly didn't mean to upset you."

Lillian could not stop crying. Like a winter storm being fed from far away northern winds, this frigid downpour seemed to have an endless supply of hurt. But not all crying makes people feel better, and in this case, it had the opposite effect. Lillian felt disgraced, and her outburst in her workplace was just another brick on the pile of her husband's offenses against her. Reinforcing herself, she said, "I'm sorry, Joanna. It's not you. It's just that my husband is very hateful."

Back in the sub shop, Joseph had just finished telling the tale of the fire-breathing dragon called Lillian. Alan said that he felt terrible for Joseph's dilemma, and rejoiced that he was no longer married. Charlie suggested that Joseph might want to get some counseling, and work on his marriage. Matt was in shock that such a likable man as Joseph could end up bound to such a completely wicked woman as Lillian.

Then Ralph unaffectedly asked the question that others were thinking but afraid to put into words, "Why not divorce?"

Everyone fell silent, awaiting the answer.

Joseph explained in generalized terms about his prenuptial agreement, and exclaimed in desperation, "I'd lose *everything*!"

Everyone noticed Alan grinning, and Ralph asked, "What's so funny, Alan?!?"

"Oh, nothing."

"It must be *something*! What is it?"

"Well," Alan leaned in to the table and lowered his voice, "What about *murder*?"

Everyone laughed anxiously, and Joseph replied, "I don't want to *lose* everything, remember? And I'm pretty sure I couldn't enjoy my life's savings in prison!"

Alan continued, "I know. I'm kidding, of course. But I read a murder mystery once where a lady got someone to kill her husband for her. When the police were going to arrest her, she turned in the killer, and walked away with the fortune."

Matt said, "Ooo, that's smart! But Joe's too good to do anything like that!"

Actually, Joseph was seriously considering the idea, but making a pretense of it outwardly said, "Any of you up for the job?" As they all laughed, Joseph added, "Oh well, 'suffering builds character,' right?"

As they returned to the office, Joseph kept hearing Alan's words, "got someone to kill, got someone to kill," echoing in his mind. He kept thinking to himself, "No! That's ridiculous, Joe! Stop thinking that!" And he tried to forget what he wanted to remember.

Lillian had just finished sharing her suffering with Joanna. Joanna had never met Joseph in person, and couldn't help envisioning him as a six-foot-six three-hundred pound ogre. After all, this was essentially how Lillian had described him. Nonetheless, Joanna wanted to encourage Lillian, but her cliché phrases sounded … well … cliché. "Hang in there! It'll be alright! It's not over 'til it's over!" and a half-dozen more truisms which offered little to console Lillian's rage.

Then Lillian spoke what Joanna was afraid to hear, "I wish he was dead!"

"No, you shouldn't say that, Lily!" Joanna protested. "Just give it some time. You can work it out. It's always darkest just before …"

Joanna's voice began to drift away as Lillian fell into imagination. She imagined arguing with Joseph in the kitchen. Joseph turned away. She calmly grabbed a knife from the drawer. Joseph was still yelling with his back toward her. She approached him unnoticed until she stood immediately behind him. She raised the knife, and in that instant Joseph turned and looked in terror as she stabbed him through the heart. As he fell to the ground, his blood stained the cabinets and the floor. "No," she thought to herself, "it's too messy." Rewinding time, she was again arguing with Joseph. He turned away, still verbally deriding her. This time she picked up a heavy cast-iron frying pan. She crept across the floor behind him, holding the pan like a medieval broadsword. Aiming for his head, and swinging with all her strength …

"Lily! Lily!!!" Joanna was snapping her fingers in front of Lillian's face. "Are you okay?!?"

"Sorry, I was distracted."

"I'll say you were! Listen, I apologize, but I have to get back to the line now. Are you sure you're going to be alright?"

"I'll be fine. I'm fine. Sorry to ruin your lunch."

"You didn't ruin anything. And if you need to talk later —about anything—just give me a call, okay?"

"Okay. Thanks, Joanna."

Lillian couldn't believe her own thoughts. She wasn't a killer, and didn't want to be a killer. How could she imagine such horrible things? And she tried to forget what she wanted to remember.

Chapter Five

At about one o'clock on Saturday afternoon, Moti was back to his routine. It had been five days since the incident at the jewelers, and despite that terrible Monday, the rest of the week actually turned out well. Four days ago, on Tuesday morning, Moti had been feeling depressed—and a little hungover. He was moving a bit slower than usual, and had to force himself to go online to check for new work. There were several pleasant surprises waiting. First, two of his regular customers had sent direct requests for his services, which meant he could now easily pay rent before tomorrow. Second, some customers had come to his defense by commenting on the negative Ross Boyd review. They said things like, "Not true … Moti is the best!" and, "Boyd won't pay? Let's Boyd-cott!" Moti didn't consider whether these comments actually affected any readers. What mattered to him was that these unsolicited words made him feel that he was no longer alone in the world. He was so encouraged that tears welled up in his eyes, as did new determination in his heart. He shook off his despair, and over the next few days, life seemed to be smiling approval and offering new hope. Those few days of steady work cleared out any remaining gloom and bills, and when he had awakened on this fresh Saturday morning, Moti's heart had felt like a white room on a Spring day with all the windows open. He casually lounged away the morning, and intended to do little else throughout the afternoon.

Suddenly—thump thump thump!—a knock at the door startled Moti from his serenity. As soon as he opened the door, he nearly fainted from shock. Two police officers with drawn weapons pushed their way into his apartment. One of them, Officer Jackson, aimed at Moti and yelled, "Up against the wall! Now! Move! Put your hands on the wall, and remain still!" Jackson maintained a fix on Moti while Officer Wilkes proceeded to thoroughly frisk him. As Moti leaned against the wall with his arms and legs sprawled, he felt like the unfortunate vermin on hunting day, hopelessly surrounded by hunters and foxhounds. Three officers waiting outside were now called in, and began moving through the apartment, but two of them were not wearing a police uniform. One of the plain-clothes officers had a camera and other photography equipment. The uniformed officer led a K—9 unit—a bloodhound—into the bedroom, bathroom, kitchen, and living room as it sniffed throughout the apartment. The third was dressed in beige slacks, and a dark blue polo shirt. Moti slowly and carefully turned his head as if his hands were glued to the wall, and tried to see what was going on in his apartment. On the back of the third officer's shirt was written in large white letters, "Homicide Detective." Moti couldn't help doing a double-take, and the quick movement of his head caused Jackson to shout, "Keep your eyes on the wall!"

Moti snapped his attention back to the wall, but said, "Officer, can someone please tell me what's going on?"

The Homicide Detective turned and said, "You are Martin Martinez, also known as 'Moti.' Is this correct?"

"Yessir, I'm Moti."

"We have a warrant. This shouldn't take long."

"A warrant? Why?!? I haven't done anything!"

"Give us just a moment, and I will explain everything."

The bloodhound was now standing in the living room, held by its leash, quietly whining and moving its head up-and-down and from side-to-side. It was apparently frustrated and dejected by its lack of success, so Wilkes suggested leading it to Moti's van. The dog seemed to understand as it started pulling its master toward the open door. Five minutes later, Moti could hear the dog outside, barking and growling. The photographer was called outside, and Moti distantly heard the camera shutter firing, cha-click! cha-click! Moti could slightly glance out the front door, and he noticed the officer walking the bloodhound away from his van with its tail wagging triumphantly. The other officer leaned in the doorway, and called, "Detective Clarke, could you come here, please?" Clarke, a middle-aged man with strikingly red hair, moved across the room, and walked outside.

Moti could vaguely hear the men talking, as well as more camera cha-click cha-click sounds. He could also hear some faint clinking noises, as if a Lilliputian was walking by with tiny keys in their tiny pockets. Detective Clarke returned wearing gloves, and holding two plastic bags. The first contained a delicate white gold necklace with a large yet elegant diamond pendant. The second contained a small sandwich bag filled with a dozen fancy rings which seemed to be set with a combination of rubies, emeralds, and diamonds.

Detective Clarke approached Moti who was still glued to the wall. Holding the bags up so Moti could see them, he asked, "Is this *all*, Martinez? Where's the rest of it?"

Moti pleaded, "The rest of *what*? I don't know what you're talking about! Where did that come from?"

"We found it inside your van, taped under dashboard on the driver's side. You probably thought the gas and oil would throw off our dog, right? A clever trick, but ineffective."

"I told you, I don't know what you're talking about! I didn't put that stuff there! I don't even know where it came from!"

Clarke nodded at Officer Jackson, who then pulled Moti's arms down from the wall, and handcuffed them behind his back. Looking at Moti, he said, "Martin

Martinez, I am arresting you for the murder of Ross Boyd."

Moti exclaimed, "Ross Boyd … murdered?!? For real?!? It wasn't me! It wasn't me!!!"

Clarke began leading Moti out of the apartment, down the thin concrete walkway, toward the empty police car waiting at the street curb. Moti walked slowly with his head down, and began to feel like all the pain and problems of his entire life had been condensed into this one unbearable experience. The loss of his biological father, the never-ending feelings of inadequacy, the inability to get ahead in life, rejection from women, and now—being arrested for murder! Moti couldn't control himself, and began bawling like a child. As Clarke and Moti approached the car, Moti began to remember his appointment with Ross a few days earlier. He felt the insults, the belittling demeanor, and the wickedness of refusing to pay. He even relived his own hatred: going to the bar, talking with G, and the meeting with Kite. Suddenly, like a reflex, Moti lifted his head with his tear-filled eyes fixed straight ahead, and mumbled, "Kite!"

Detective Clarke heard Moti quite clearly, and a troubled look covered his face as he examined Moti's countenance. Clarke looked around to see if any of the other officers were in earshot. Fortunately, he and Moti were now standing near the police car outside, safely distanced from the others. Clarke questioned, "I'm sure I heard you say, 'Kite'! Is that correct?!?"

Moti was like a man shaken from sleep. He had been so consumed in his own thoughts that he had forgotten that he was in handcuffs with the detective. Moti breathed to tell the story when it occurred to him that attempting to hire a hitman to kill someone who was just murdered might not help his defense. He simply said, "Nothing. I didn't say nothing. I was just thinking."

Clarke could sense Moti's resistance, and wanted to earn his confidence. Officer Wilkes was approaching and already half-way to the car, and Officer Jackson was closing up the apartment. Clarke had no time for private conversation. He looked intently into Moti's eyes and said with the seriousness of a surgeon, "Mister Martinez, do *not* mention 'Kite' to *anyone* besides me. I strongly urge this for your own safety. Do you understand?"

Moti was in utter confusion. Was this man who was wrongfully arresting him now concerned for his safety? Impossible! Or perhaps this was not a warning at all— was it actually a threat? Despite all doubts, something in Clarke's eyes communicated such intelligent sincerity that Moti was compelled to simply nod in submission. Clarke decided to follow the officers carrying Moti to the police station, and to personally witness the entire booking. At the station, Clarke insisted that Moti was a suicide risk, and that he must be placed in a cell with round-the-clock audio and video surveillance.

Moti protested, "Suicide risk?!? You're crazy if you think ..."

Clarke interrupted, "Be quiet, Martinez! Just know that I'm not going to let any harm come to you—unless you're found guilty."

Moti sat there with his mouth open, too confused to speak. He couldn't understand if Clarke was truly concerned for him, or just content to torment him with double-talk. But some indescribable instinct made Moti feel that he should trust this moody detective. Suddenly, the booking officer stepped away for a moment leaving Clarke and Moti alone at the desk. Clarke spoke in hushed tones, and pulling out a small scratchpad and pencil urged Moti, "Your only hope of safety is to tell me the *truth*! Do you understand?!? Tell me *facts*—any names or places that I can investigate. Do it quickly!!!"

Moti whispered as Clarke scratched down notes, "I went to a bar, I'm not sure about the name. I think it was 'Handsome Tavern,' or something like that. I was ... well, I guess I was too angry and drunk to pay attention. Some guy called 'G' took me to some scary guy named Kite—but I didn't ... I mean ... I was drunk, and thinking stupid!" Then the shame of all that had happened caused his head to hang, and he whimpered, "My own hate has destroyed me."

The booking officer returned, finished the paperwork, and Moti was escorted to his cell. To ensure Moti's safety, Clarke shrewdly reiterated to the surveillance staff that Moti might be suicidal and should never be taken to a non-monitored area without at least two officers present.

Chapter Six

The body of Ross Boyd had been discovered a few hours earlier by Eric and Gale Winkler, a husband-wife cleaning service. Every Saturday, they would arrive at the jewelry store at five-thirty in the morning, enter through the back door, disable the alarm system, and perform their cleaning duties. They told police that when they arrived, they knew something was wrong. The alarm system had not been activated, "and Mister Boyd would *never* forget to activate it." With such foreboding, Gale grabbed her mop handle like a sword, Eric wielded a squeegee pole, and they began to cautiously walk through the store. When they reached the showroom, Mister Boyd's body was lying on the floor with a gun in his left hand and a note in his right. They touched nothing, and immediately called the police. But although Ross appeared to have shot himself, in the hysteria of the moment, Mister Winkler only told the emergency operator, "Mister Boyd's been shot! He's been shot!!!"

Officer Jacobs was nearby on his beat, and was the first to arrive on the scene. Within an hour after, Homicide Detective William Clarke arrived. At first glance, this looked like a suicide, and Clarke was a bit miffed at having been called for something that was clearly outside his field. While the crime scene photographer was busy, Clarke went looking through the store for

Jacobs to complain about being called. Jacobs was in Ross's personal office looking at a framed photograph that was hanging on the wall. Clarke began to scold him, "This appears to be a suicide, Jacobs. Why did you call *me* here?"

Jacobs glanced at him, then fixed his eyes back on the photo. He calmly answered with a question, "Have you seen the body?"

"Of course I've seen the body!" Clarke retorted.

"And why do you think it's suicide?"

"Because he was clutching a *note*."

"In which hand?"

Clarke stopped to think, "In his *right* hand."

Jacobs continued, "Correct. And the gun was in his *left* hand."

"So what's your point, Jacobs?" Clarke demanded.

"Look carefully at this photo on the wall."

There were four men in the photo, all of which were dressed in camouflage and messy with paint. One of them was clearly Ross Boyd, probably a few years earlier. Each man was holding their paintball gun victoriously in the air, and Clarke assumed they must've been the champions of that day's paintball battle. Then he noticed that Ross had lifted his paintball gun in his *right* hand.

Clarke grinned at Jacobs, and said, "The gun's in the wrong hand. Good job, Jacobs! You'll have *my* job before long! This may be a homicide after all, and if so, a clever culprit to boot."

Jacobs said solemnly, "I actually don't deserve your praise. I think I know who the murderer is, and he's a man that I personally let go. I was called here a few days ago for a disturbance. This carpet-cleaner guy was making a scene in the store claiming that Boyd had ripped him off. I personally heard him say he wanted to kill Boyd, and I ended up cuffing him and leading him out of the store. At the time, I didn't think the guy was really a killer—he looked like the kind of man you usually don't take too seriously. And when Boyd didn't press charges, I had to let him go. Still, I filed a police report, and I remember that his name was Martin Martinez."

Clarke was taking notes, and paused as he jested, "Martin Martinez? Well, we can't give his parents high marks for creativity."

Jacobs grinned, and said, "Also, he has a strange nickname ... what was it? Oh yes, it's 'Moti.' But I'll tell you something, Clarke—he didn't strike me as being smart enough to stage something like this. I suppose he sure fooled me."

Clarke removed the photo as evidence, as well as some handwritten sticky notes discovered on Boyd's desk. The men left the office, and proceeded to the crime scene where Clarke donned some latex gloves, and carefully removed the note from Boyd's lifeless hand. Comparing the note to the samples from Boyd's desk, Clarke commented, "I have to admit, Jacobs, I think you're correct about this being a homicide. The two handwriting samples have such obvious discrepancies that it's *impossible* that Boyd wrote this suicide note. This is a pretty sloppy attempt to fake a suicide, so I must thank this 'Moti' character when we meet."

Jacobs was no rookie, but this irony forced even him to question the detective, "*Thank* him? What for?"

"For making my job so easy," Clarke quipped.

Clarke's personal philosophy made him a man in search of justice and truth. He had long believed that, because he sought goodness, his efforts must produce goodness. In other words, because he wanted justice, he believed he was causing justice. In this case, the evidence against Moti was conclusive, and Clarke's intentions were pure. Therefore, by arresting, trying, and sentencing Moti, justice would be accomplished. The only snags in this philosophy were those arrested who protested their innocence. In these cases, Clarke justified himself based upon the evidence. If the evidence was irrefutable—and Clarke had been objective in his investigation and interpretation of that evidence—then he believed that justice would always prevail. This gave him unusual self-confidence and pride in his work. The only stain on his otherwise clean conscience was the Darrell case six months ago.

Frank Darrell had owned a local hardware store for more than twenty years. The police report said that almost seven thousand dollars in cash had disappeared from the safe, along with an estimated twenty-one thousand dollars worth of products. Darrell was reportedly suspicious that his store manager, Daniel Pole, was the culprit of these thefts. This report was based upon an email that was sent from Darrell's computer confronting Pole for stealing these items, and threatening him if they were not returned. The next day, Pole's body was found, and Clarke had personally arrested Darrell for the murder.

Darrell denied all involvement, and said, "None of your evidence is *real*! I never wrote that email, and Dan never stole anything from me! Why can't you see that?!? I know who framed me—and who killed Dan. But if I mention his name, I won't survive the week—not even in jail! You'll think I killed myself, but I would *never* kill myself! Anyone who mentions 'Kite' to the cops never survives."

Less than forty-eight hours later, Darrell's body was found hanging in his cell. He had used his pants as a rope.

Clarke had struggled with Darrell's death. The black-and-white absolutes that supplied his confidence were being shaken by shades of gray. For the first time in his career, he felt unsure of himself. He couldn't forget the words, "I would *never* kill myself!" If that was true, then Darrell was innocent. And if Darrell was innocent, then Clarke felt he had inadvertently contributed to his death. But even if Darrell hadn't died in jail, if he was innocent, that would mean that Clarke had arrested him based on evidence that had been falsified. And Clarke knew himself well enough to know that he would have energetically assisted the prosecution against Darrell.

Clarke's mission in life—in a practical sense—was to serve *Justitia*, the goddess of justice who stood blindfolded, with scales and sword in hand. But in his pursuit for blind justice, was he merely running blind? Was he actually hurting the *innocent*? How many others had he wrongfully hurt? These questions had thrown Clarke into a sort of identity crisis which he had not been able to resolve.

The only clue he had to the mystery of Darrell's death—and the goads upon his conscience—was the name, "Kite." But lacking any more leads or evidence, he was forced to bottle up the memory, and place it on a shelf in his mind.

Chapter Seven

On the suburban street where the Brightons lived, each household seemed to reserve Saturday afternoon for their particular family activity. For instance, the Parker family—two doors down, and cater-cornered to the left —they spent their Saturday afternoons in outdoor activities such as going the park, barbecuing, and playing frisbee. The Hitchcocks—who lived on the corner—always used Saturday to play their music loud enough for the entire neighborhood to enjoy with them. And the Wisenbergs next door were always in the driveway of their house every Saturday, washing and waxing their three cars.

Like many people, Joseph and Lillian were keenly aware of their neighbor's habits while being completely oblivious to their own. Thus, they knew well the aforementioned customs, but didn't realize how they were known to their neighbors: for using Saturdays to argue and scream at each other. And since this was an ordinary weekend in the neighborhood, the Wisenbergs next door were outside polishing wheels and windows, pretending not to listen as they heard the Brightons shouting inside their home.

Lillian raged, "You're so selfish! I bought that for *me*!!!"

Joseph retaliated, "It was sitting in the refrigerator all week! I ate it so it wouldn't go bad!"

"It was a microwaveable meal, Joe! They *never* go bad!"

"Excuse me for being hungry! Sheesh! You act like I should starve!"

"Here we go! It's the Joe-can't-stick-to-the-point-when-he's-wrong show!"

"I know the point! You won't be happy until I'm dead!!!"

"As far as I'm concerned, you can drop dead right now!!!"

Ding dong! Thump thump thump! In the middle of their last exchange, a visitor had approached their house, rung the doorbell, and quite loudly knocked on the door. Joseph and Lillian looked at each other embarrassed, and Joseph ran to look out the front window.

"There's a police car out front!" he whispered back to Lillian who was fixing her appearance.

Joseph opened the door cautiously, "Can I help you?"

The man replied, "My name is Will Clarke. I'm with the Homicide Investigation Division of the Metro Police."

Joseph nervously interrupted, "Did someone call the cops?!? Sorry Officer, no one's been hurt. We were just having an argument, that's all."

Clarke laughed, "No one called, sir. I'm here to ask you some questions about a friend of yours, Mister Martin Martinez."

Joseph and Lillian looked at each other with concern, and Lillian stepped forward, "You mean Moti? Is he alright?"

"I'm sorry, ma'am, but Mister Martinez has been arrested on suspicion of murder."

Joseph exclaimed defensively, "That's absurd! Moti's the kind of guy who feeds pigeons and sparrows, and takes home stray dogs. He doesn't have the constitution to commit murder!"

Clarke replied, "That's actually why I'm here. Your friend, Moti—Mister Martinez, that is—provided your names as character witnesses. It's completely voluntary on your part."

Joseph and Lillian exchanged a glance, and Joseph stepped aside as he said, "Of course, come in and have a seat. Anything we can do to help."

Joseph sat in his favorite chair, Lillian sat alone on the love-seat, and Detective Clarke was surprised at having the entire sofa to himself.

Clarke began, "I am going to be candid with both of you in hopes that you will both be candid with me. I have a standard procedure for my investigations that has served me well. But Mister Martinez's case has some unusual aspects that are forcing me to bend my own rules. Therefore, I'll tell you up front what I would normally never tell you: I personally believe what you said about your friend, and I do not believe that he is the killer. I believe that he may become another victim of the actual murderer. But I need *evidence* if I am to prove this in court."

Joseph and Lillian were visibly nervous, and Lillian only managed to peep out, "What do you want from us?"

Clarke asked, "Are you familiar with the 'Handsome Tavern,' or something like that?"

They both shook their heads.

Clarke continued, "It's a bar where Mister Martinez went a few days before the murder."

Joseph looked frustrated, and said, "Detective Clarke, I'm sorry, but you're not making sense. Who was murdered? When did it happen? And how did Moti get mixed up in it?"

Clarke apologized, "Yes, you're right. That's what I get for abandoning my procedures. Let me fill you in properly." He proceeded to tell them what he knew of the story: Martinez was hired by Boyd, Boyd refused to pay, Martinez hysterically returned to the store, and the police heard Martinez exclaim that he would kill Boyd. At this point, Clarke's own thoughts interrupted his speech. He looked up like a pirate who had just found a chest of gold, opened his notebook, and frantically scribbled some notes to himself. Then he calmly proceeded to explain, "Martinez told me he was so depressed after being arrested that he went to a bar called 'Handsome Tavern,' or something like that. He wasn't certain of the name, and couldn't remember where it was located. Apparently, he met someone there named 'G' who introduced him to someone I believe to be a hitman."

Lillian exclaimed, "A hitman?!?"

"Yes," replied Clarke, "and it is this man that I believe is responsible for the murder of Ross Boyd, as well as the framing of your friend. If I'm correct, he uses the name 'Kite' for his nefarious affairs."

Joseph chuckled, "Does he hang people by a little string, and fly in the air?"

Clarke scowled his disapproval, "This is not a joke, Mister Brighton. And I assume the name is a reference to the bird of prey."

"Sorry," Joseph bleated, "you're right. This is serious."

Lillian seemed to be lost in thought, and was looking at her mobile phone as she said, "Hemlock! I'll bet it was Hemlock Tavern!"

Clarke and Joseph both looked questioningly at Lillian then each other. She explained, "I checked my internet map for bars, and a few miles away is a place called Hemlock Tavern. It's the only bar that's name is even remotely similar."

Clarke smiled with some embarrassment, "Missus Brighton, that was a good idea. I checked criminal databases, and even attempted phonetic matching. But in my haste, I failed to use common sense. Thank you."

Lillian blushed at the compliment, then asked, "So what can we do now?"

Clarke stood up to leave, and said, "You've done enough for now, but I need to get back to work. This interview has provided me with a crucial lead, as well as sparked some ideas of my own. I appreciate your time."

Joseph led Clarke outside to his car, and the Wisenbergs took a break from their carwash to satisfy their curiosity as to whether or not their neighbor was under arrest. Joseph paused behind the car to ask, "What about Moti? When is his trial? Can we visit him?"

"Right now, only immediate family can visit. But I will tell him to add you to his visitors list, and I'll contact you once you are able." And to the Wisenberg's disappointment, Clarke entered his police car and drove away alone.

Joseph walked slowly back to the front door with his head and eyes downward, not noticing how enthusiastically the Wisenberg's were now scrubbing their tires. His attention was elsewhere, but distantly he thought he heard a sound like Lillian's voice, and it was crying. He entered the house, closed the door behind him, then followed the sound through the hall to their bedroom. In the past few years, he had developed an almost inhumane and mocking cynicism toward her tears. Every time she cried, he felt that she was attempting to manipulate some primal instinct inside him, the desire to rescue the damsel in distress. He had decidedly hardened his heart, and would allow it no more.

He stood in the doorway of the bedroom, crossed his arms, and leaned on the doorframe. There was Lillian, laying on the bed crying. Looking at Lillian with suspicion he asked, "What's wrong with you *now*?"

Lillian sat up, and fired back with painful anger in her eyes, "I was just thinking of Moti, and how unfair life is. I'm just sick of it! I'm sick of life! I'm sick of you! For one day before I die, I'd like to feel *happy* again! I don't even remember what it was like! I'm just sick of it all! I hate it! And I blame *you*!!!"

Joseph was unaffected, and was certain that everything she said was simply dramatic lies. Her *real* motives, he thought, were to break him down, to get him to lower his guard, to exploit him, and to take advantage. He drolly replied, "That's nice dear. But the show's over now, so let's lose the drama. Okay?"

Lillian's hatred raged into a scream. She jumped off the bed with her fists in the air, and charged at Joseph in a furious fit. As she swung for his head, Joseph intercepted both of her arms in his hands and held on tightly. He had never seen her behave like this, and he was both surprised and scared. He shouted, "You crazy witch! Get ahold of yourself! The police just left—do you want me to call them back?!?"

These words had a profound effect on her, but not for the reason that Joseph supposed. She relaxed her arms so Joseph would release her, then she calmly walked back to the bed and sat down. She explained, "I don't know what came over me. I'm just very upset right now. Just leave me alone!"

"Gladly!" Joseph snorted, and walked out to his living room chair. As he sat there, he began talking to himself. "She's losing her mind! I'm sure of it! My God, I never thought she'd get *physical*. I'm not sure it's even safe to sleep here anymore. I'll be darned if I'm going to live like this. She can't treat *me* like this!" Then he had a truly horrible thought. He seemed to shake it off, but then it recurred with more plausibility. Joseph pulled out his mobile phone, opened up his internet map, and searched for "Hemlock Tavern."

If it's true that great minds think alike, then it's reasonable that wicked minds do the same. Lillian watched Joseph as he walked away from the bedroom, and immediately picked up her phone. The map was still open and displaying the location of the Hemlock Tavern. Lillian need not speak, for the ill will in her eyes declared her intent.

Chapter Eight

At about three o'clock that afternoon, Joseph put on some jeans, a teeshirt, and—although he disliked hats—a baseball cap. He was secretly a little vain about his hair being neat, and despised hat hair, bed head, and the feeling of his hair being windblown. Like the tensing of a coiled snake, this small change in his behavior was the telltale flexing of something deadly in his soul. After Lillian's outburst that morning, she had remained in the bedroom all day and eventually fell asleep in emotional exhaustion. Unaffected, Joseph walked to the garage, and got into his car as casually as if he was running an errand. But this was a trip like none other he'd taken before, and a fall from which most never return.

He drove past the *Hemlock Tavern* by mistake the first time. The signpost was bent near the bottom, and looked as if some drunk must've run into it after one too many at the bar. This caused the sign to be very easy to see from one direction, and nearly impossible to see from Joseph's approach. By the time he could read it, he was already past it. In that infinitesimal moment when Joseph realized that he had missed it, an entire battle was waged in his conscience. He thought that maybe *missing the sign* was *a sign*—some form of divine intervention to keep him from his purpose. Then he thought about Lillian's rage that morning, and exaggerated his own fears of her violence to justify himself. He saw the damaged signpost, and his damaged marriage. He wondered why the post hadn't been repaired, and concluded that it was beyond repair —it must be torn down and replaced! And with the confidence of this momentary madness, he quickly turned around, and drove back to the tavern.

Inside was more crowded than Joseph had expected for a Saturday afternoon. In the corners of the room near the ceiling were mounted cheap speakers. These not only filled the room with a variety of ambient music, but also prevented the conversations of others from being easily overheard. Once his eyes adjusted to the light, Joseph instinctively applied his attention to detail, and quickly analyzed the several patrons. He created three categories in his mind: the drunks, the drinkers, and the thugs. First, the "drunks" were those who wore dirty or sloppy clothing. Second, the "drinkers" were dressed more neatly, but were obviously there for the liquor. And finally, the "thugs" were standing or seated alone, and were physically intimidating. At the moment, the room only contained two men in the "thug" category, one standing at the side of the room with his massive arms crossed, and one seated at the bar. Joseph walked up to the bar, and took a seat. He wasn't interested in drinking, but ordered a beer for the look of the thing. He looked at the thug who seemed to be watching back in his peripheral vision.

Joseph said, "How you doing?"

The thug never turned, but simply replied, "Sss-up?"

Joseph said, "I need some help."

Still looking forward, "This ain't a charity."

Joseph leaned slightly, and whispered, "I've got a 'people problem,' and I'm looking for Kite."

At the mention of *Kite*, the thug was visibly startled, and looked directly at Joseph, then examined the room to make sure no one else had overheard. After a brief pause, he cautiously replied, "Who's that?"

Joseph stood to his feet, and said, "I suppose you're the wrong person, I'll just …"

The thug looked around to room to ensure that they weren't drawing any attention, and whispered, "Cool your heels, dog, and let's talk—quiet like. I'm G."

G held a horizontal fist in the air, and Joseph stared curiously for a moment until he realized—he fist-bumped and sat down. G questioned Joseph for a few minutes until he was satisfied that Joseph was a sincere —and solvent—client. Then he explained the necessity of taking a blindfolded ride. After Joseph agreed, G pulled out his phone, and sent a message on ahead.

This wicked adventure was throbbing through Joseph's heart and head like a jackhammer. They exited the bar, walked around to the back, and he climbed into one of the two white vehicles parked there. Although G proceeded to blindfold him, Joseph's detail-oriented mind attempted to map out the trip by timing the straights, and counting the turns. It seemed to him that after driving approximately two minutes to the north, they had actually made three right turns, all about a minute apart. Then after another two minutes to the west, they made another three right turns about a minute apart. Then after two minutes south, they made three left turns about a minute apart. Then they made a quick left-left-right before they turned left into a garage. If the map in his brain was correct, this meant that they were actually in a neighborhood quite close to their starting position.

G led Joseph into the meeting room, and systematically sat him down and exited the room. Sitting there blind, Joseph sensed another presence in the room, now moving behind him.

"Is someone there?" Joseph asked.

"Yes, I am," replied Kite in his contradictory tone. As he loosened and removed the blindfold, he continued, "And so are you, Joseph Brighton of 749 Croaster Road."

Joseph's shock and fear were readily visible, as was Kite's gratification at the reaction. Kite walked around Joseph, toward the desk in front of him, and continued imperiously, "You work as a Director of Finance, you have been married for ten years, you have no children, and a 'people problem' for which you need my assistance: Missus Lillian Brighton, I believe." Joseph's fixed stare irritated Kite's condescension so that he shouted, "Mister Brighton! Are you listening?!? The Package is the insufferable Missus Lillian Brighton, yes or no?!?"

Between being shaken by Kite's shouts, and hearing Lillian's hateful name, Joseph shook off his better self and confirmed confidently, "Yes."

Kite calmly proceeded, "So, to brass tacks. Since you can't distance yourself from the Package, you must strive to divert any suspicion. I suggest that you spend the next three months demonstrating to those around you how devoted you are to your wife. The delivery will then happen, and no one will have cause to suspect you."

Joseph protested, "But I can't stand her! What am I supposed to do?!?"

"Send her flowers—or chocolates—when she's at work, so *others see it*. Take her on a double-date with friends so *others see it*. *Pretend* to be devoted so *others see it*! Understand?"

Joseph began to speak in disgust, "Send flowers! I don't think …"

"It's either that or a jail cell, Mister Brighton! And since I don't get my second payment if you're arrested, I have a vested interest in making sure you're not even suspected. Do you understand?!?"

Joseph reluctantly uttered, "Yes, I understand."

"Now then, speaking of payment," Kite continued, "a delivery is twenty thousand dollars, fifty percent up front, and fifty percent precisely ten days after delivery." Just then Kite's phone beeped with a message, and he chuckled out loud as he silently read the text to himself.

When Joseph had left the house earlier, Lillian was just waking. She sat up in bed just as he closed the garage door, and in her groggy state she could hear him drive away. She picked up her phone to check the time, and saw the map to the Hemlock Tavern. Some think of sleep as a panacea, and say things like, "just sleep on it," or "you'll feel better after a good night's sleep." But sleep usually works best for those who believe, "do not allow the sun to go down when you're angry." Lillian, however, had gone to sleep in the wet cement of her anger, and had awoke more hardened in her heart. Staring at the map—and especially the word *hemlock*—she spoke out loud, "I'm going!"

She thought ahead about entering a strange tavern by herself, and decided that she didn't want to attract any unwanted attention from the patrons. Therefore, she forced herself to wash off all of her makeup, and tied her hair up in what she considered to be an unattractive bun. She dressed in loose-fitting sweatpants, an oversized teeshirt, and sneakers. Under normal circumstances she would never allow herself to leave the house in such a state. But these were not normal circumstances. In fact, her homely air coupled with the hatred emanating from her face were synergistic in making this otherwise attractive woman appear utterly hideous.

Her thoughts were a million miles away during the drive to the tavern. If not for the GPS announcing directions, she would have driven right by. In her heightened nervousness, she quickly parked and entered the building, taking no notice of any other vehicles, not even her husband's. Because G was away with a client, another of Kite's cronies was in his spot at the bar. Lillian had remembered the name "G" from the meeting with Detective Clarke. Her first thought was to ask the bartender for help. The bartender was a middle-aged woman attempting to look young, and a forced smile that provoked both pity and pain. The closer Lillian got, the more offensive this woman seemed to her. The lines under her eyes looked like desert washes, patterned with the mud of thick foundation makeup. Her teeth seemed to be the pillars at Stonehenge, gapped and stained brownish gray from years of tobacco and drug use. Her hair, which seemed so beautiful at a glance, when viewed up-close, was a clearly aging wig. Lillian shuttered to think what lay beneath it, and her disgust was written on her face.

The bartender obliviously smiled, "What can I get'cha, Hun?"

Lillian lowered her voice and leaned over the bar, "I'm looking for G."

The bartender leaned over the counter and examined Lillian like a judge at a beauty contest, and said, "Well, you're not his usual type, are you? But it's no matter 'cuz he ain't here. You just missed him."

At the end of the bar was another large-armed thug who had been watching Lillian from the moment she entered. He spoke up softly, "I'll take it from here, Candy."

Candy replied, "Suit yourself," and went back to work at the other end of the bar.

Lillian felt like a dwarf before this colossus, and fearfully peeped out, "Are you G?" having momentarily forgotten that he was not there.

"No, but I work with him. I'm T." T grinned mockingly and said, "You don't look like anyone that G usually hangs with, unless he's slummin'!" Then he burst out in deep laughter at his own joke while Lillian sheepishly looked around the room to see who might be looking. Like dynamite puts out oil well fires, T's laughter was suddenly quenched as he saw Lillian's hidden fire flare up in her eyes. "Sorry," he said, reseating himself upright. "What'dya need?"

"You said you work with G, is that right?" Lillian asked.

"That's right."

"Well, I heard that G might know someone who can help *take care* of people. Do you know someone like that?"

T's demeanor became surprisingly stoic, and he subtly nodded affirmation. He began to question Lillian about her situation, and eventually agreed to take her to Kite. He explained the necessity of blindfolding her for the ride, and Lillian's fear of vulnerability was evident.

"You don't need to worry," T comforted her, "we're a *delivery* service, not *thieves*." He again laughed at his own joke. "Besides, I will be your personal bodyguard while you're in my care. No one will lay a finger on you, or I'll bust 'em up." And he flexed his frightening fists.

If Lillian had been thinking rationally, she wouldn't have had cause to trust anything that T told her as being reliable. But despite his criminality, she was convinced that he would protect her. This thought worked to fuel her hatred against her husband even more since—as she believed—he had left her so alone and unprotected against the world. She accompanied T to a white S.U.V.

behind the tavern, and he took her blindfolded to Kite's home. Upon entering, the blindfolded Lillian heard someone tell T, "He's got a client back there, should be done soon." So T gently pulled Lillian's arms to direct her into a chair, and told her, "Just sit here quietly for about five minutes. Not a word, understand?" Lillian nodded. Then T exclaimed, "Dang it! I forgot to text him!" and quickly typed a message on his phone.

Kite grinned as he looked from his phone to Joseph, and Joseph confusedly grinned back. Kite dismissed the message, and put his phone back in his pocket. After providing details of a particular charity where Joseph could make the "donations," Kite replaced the blindfold and texted G to come retrieve him for transport back to the tavern. G warned Joseph that there was another client in the house, and that Joseph was not to make a sound until they were back at the tavern.

When T was summoned, he directed Lillian to stand and wait. G emerged from the meeting room, guiding the blindfolded Joseph. G looked at T and said, "Move out of the way, or we can't pass!" So T gently pulled Lillian's arms to get her out of the way of Joseph. Even when they passed within a foot of each other, they were worlds apart.

As Joseph left the tavern he felt an evil euphoria like that of a cruel child burning insects under a magnifying glass. He was so self-indulged that he took no notice of Lillian's car at the tavern. He was outwardly lighthearted, and as he drove away, he buried himself by singing along with the hit songs on the radio. With his nerves now settling, his stomach began to grumble, and he decided to treat himself to dinner before returning home.

As Lillian was seated in Kite's office, she could hear someone tapping away at a computer. Ordinarily, Kite liked the suspense produced by silence when receiving new clients, and would not speak until they had first moved or spoken. This time was different.

Kite continued to tap at the computer and said, "Just a moment, and I'll be right with you. We're having a large volume of calls today, so your expected wait time is about thirty seconds." And then he chuckled.

Lillian actually felt a sense of disappointment. She had expected some frightful and intelligent killer, and this tranquil voice was more comforting than intimidating. A moment later, Kite removed the blindfold, and Lillian couldn't hide the letdown. She raised one eyebrow, and asked suspiciously, "*You're* Kite?"

Kite now realized his error in not producing the proper mood to begin with. He sat down at his desk, and calmly spoke, "Yes, I am. And you are Missus Lillian Brighton of 749 Croaster Road. You are the office manager at All Products Electronics, you have no children, and you want to hire me to fix a problem you have with your husband, the insufferable Mister Joseph Brighton. But perhaps you've changed your mind?"

Kite's flaming arrow hit its mark, and Lillian's mouth literally fell open. She began to speak, "No! No, I don't want to change my mind! But how ..."

Kite interrupted, "Never mind. You just need to know that I am very good at what I do, but I am not above offense. So, to brass tacks." Kite first explained Lillian's need to distance herself from suspicion by displaying before others her utter devotion to her husband.

Lillian asked, "How do I *display* my devotion?"

Kite placidly responded, "I'm sure I don't know, Missus Brighton. But I'm sure a clever woman like you will think of something. Now, regarding payment. Ordinarily, a delivery is twenty thousand, with fifty percent up front, and fifty percent ten days after delivery. But in your situation, it might complicate things if your husband was to stumble upon your withdrawal. Therefore, I want to propose something better for you. I want to suggest that you could create a temporary *will*, and in it you will stipulate that all of your assets will go to my 'charity.' Then, after the delivery is made—and any dust has settled—then you can 'donate' the twenty, and change your will back however you'd like. This means that you can get what you want without any suspicion, and it's no problem for me to wait a few extra days to accommodate you."

Lillian very much liked the sound of "no suspicion," so much that any other terms seemed moot in comparison. She quickly agreed, and after another blindfolded ride, found herself driving home with a sinister and victorious look in her eye.

Now alone in his office, Kite leaned back in his chair, and put his hands on the back of his head with triumphant arrogance. Looking up at the ceiling, and thinking out loud he said, "Kite, you lucky and clever devil! Both come to you to bump each other off, and *you alone* are going to end up with all their assets! I'll knock off both of them—when they're *together*—and make it look like an accident. And when that woman's new will is read, the entire estate will pass to my charity … to *me*! Absolutely brilliant!!!" And although he laughed, he wasn't joking.

Chapter Nine

Clarke had spent Sunday completely removed from the burdens of his work. It was a discipline of self-preservation and professional detachment which he had forced upon himself early in his career. But every Monday morning he would pick up those burdens again, and strap them on like a mountain climber's pack prepared for a month in the wilderness. On this Monday, one could almost see him bend over under the weight of his thoughts as he began to ponder the mystery of the Boyd case. He had driven to the office early, and had been sitting at his desk supporting his head with his hands while reviewing his notes from the Brighton interview. His desk was in the corner of a large room filled with several other desks where field officers and other detectives would process their own paperwork. He always felt fortunate to have the corner workstation because it was the most out-of-the-way location in what could sometimes be a very crowded environment. He saw what he had scribbled not two days before, while talking to the Brightons: "Martinez case like Darrell? Who killed Darrell? Mole?!?" The words were cryptic, but he knew what they meant. And as suspicions of one of his greatest fears began to rise in his heart, he whispered to himself, "Who could've known about Martinez' threats against Boyd, and been able to get the info to this Kite person between the time that Martinez left the bar, and arrived at the house? It could only be someone *here*, in the station … a *mole*! I need to find out who was here at that time, but first …"

Clarke jumped up and went over to his personal filing cabinets. He pulled the Manila file folders containing the documents from these two parallel cases: Martinez and Darrell. He began to review the files from both cases, hoping to find a common thread. Perhaps, he thought, there was one particular person who was somehow involved in both arrests. Perhaps some shared feature that seemed unimportant at the time would now reveal an important clue. He created an accurate list of the names of all persons involved in the Darrell file, and then a similar list of names from the Martinez file. But to his utter disappointment, the only commonality was *himself*. His thoughts were soon interrupted by a paranoid terror: "if someone else was doing this investigation, they might think that *I* was a mole!" But he quickly realized these thoughts were counterproductive, and forced them out of mind.

He continued going through each folder, reviewing each page, examining every apparent detail. In the Martinez folder, he began to review the original police report that he had inherited from Officer Jacobs, describing Moti's tantrum at the jewelers. As he turned the page, something caught his attention. A short black hair was clinging there, contrasted against the white paper, held by a minuscule static charge. Clarke was about to instinctively blow it away when he quickly stopped, and held his breath. Jacobs had thin blonde hair, which was cut medium length. What was this hair doing here, and to whom did it belong? Without breathing, he slowly reached in his desk to get an evidence collection envelope and tweezers. He carefully collected the hair from the page, and sealed it in the envelope. Excited by this discovery, he cautiously went through each file again looking for more potential evidence. But after a few minutes of meticulous searching, he found none. Despite this, he held up the envelope triumphantly, and headed off to the Forensics Biology unit.

Clarke knew that, unlike crime fiction, DNA testing was not magic, and it was not instant. Each step of the process required the interpretation of specialists, as well as a review by their peers. And then a match would still have to be located in the Combined DNA Index System, known as CODIS. Unless he somehow got lucky, the entire process could normally take several weeks to complete. Rather than allow this to discourage him, Clarke used this as a motivation to get the process started without any delay. Once that was underway, he would start gathering information about the Hemlock Tavern.

Early Tuesday morning, the tavern was closed and the front parking lot empty. But if you listened carefully, you could hear faint noises coming from around the back. In the trash dumpster, empty bottles clinked together, and plastic bags slowly rustled. Like the disturbed waters of the black deep before a breaching whale, the garbage bubbled aside before this emerging creature. Strenuous grunts and groans could be heard as a dirty hand appeared on the dumpster wall like the claw of a zombie from a dirty grave, grabbing at any hold, pulling itself back to the land of the living. From outside the dumpster, all that could be seen was two arms suddenly thrown over the edge, clamping the wall at the armpit, and a head soon appearing, clamping the wall at the chin. The head was topped with a battered boonie hat, and the face was almost entirely covered with a matted beard of about seven days growth. The eyes had not yet opened, but squinted tight from the pain caused by the recent sunrise. Another groan provoked a comforting hand to move to the ailing head, now suffering from the contents drained from the bottles during the previous night. The few people who knew the head called it Harold, along with the rest of him.

Harold struggled out of the dumpster, and staggered toward the back of the tavern. He grabbed the chain that was clipped to his belt-loop, and draped into his back pocket. As he carefully tugged, the chain slowly emerged like a snake-charmer's pet, until the loose end popped out, holding a key. Attached to the back of the tavern was a locked bathroom to which Harold had been granted access, and which he now fumbled to open. Half of the reason for this convenience was that

Harold was expected to keep his eyes and ears open for anything unusual, and report it. The other half, no one at the tavern understood for certain, except that it was a mercy provided on behalf of something from Harold's past. Harold received other perks, as well, in the form of expiring food-stuffs from the tavern, and a weekly allowance of booze, which he euphemized as his "medicine." But rather than make him well, this *hair of the dog* only made him more sick.

Today's hangover throbbed Harold's brain like a machine gun, and as he reached up to comfort his head with both hands, he accidentally touched his disfigured right ear. For a moment, his eyes opened wide, and his sun-dried face became a moistened pallor. Then overwhelming memories usurped his consciousness, and forced him to fall sobbing to his knees.

It was February 1991, and the hammering of machine guns filled his ears and soul. Private Harold Harrison was part of a ground assault to liberate Kuwait from Iraqi troops. Although of timid nature, the shock and terror of combat had awakened in him an unusual form of courage. It was not the courage of a rational soldier performing justice in defending a weak people from a strong oppressor. It was the courage of a panicked and cornered beast, the last-ditch fight instinct of a creature that had lost all sense of hope. Moments earlier, Harold had been hugging his assault rifle like a long-lost child recently found, when he saw a soldier to the left take a bullet in the head and fall lifeless to the ground. He had just met the man, Private James, a few days earlier, and they had begun to become friends. Now James' corpse lay staring at Harold, accusing his cowardice, begging for vengeance. The initial fright and the following horror were soon displaced by a mindless rage. The battle had now turned, and the enemy were breaking formation in a wild retreat. But Harold's fervor and fearful fury were just reaching their peak, and he leapt up out the trench, screaming and shooting.

To the right, Sergeant Gunther's attention was drawn by Harold's battlecry, and he shouted back, "Harrison! Get back here! Get down!!!"

Harold could hear his voice, but it sounded miles away, buried by the gunfire, hidden by the battle smoke. Harold saw the enemy running at a distance, their backs toward him. But his thoughts were still in chaos, and he kept shooting, watching his victims fall, shot in the back. Then—whizzzz, pop! This strange sound was followed by pain from his right ear, then a dripping on his neck. He kept shooting, but to the right he could faintly hear shouting voices.

Gunther cried out to another nearby soldier, "Wilkes! Give me cover fire!"

Wilkes acknowledged, "You got it, Sarge!"

Gunther screamed, "Now!!!"

As Private Wilkes began laying down cover, Sergeant Gunther ran over and tackled Harrison for his own safety. Harrison looked up in a state of shock, reached for the pain on his ear, and then passed out. The battle had quickly wound down, and Gunther and Wilkes carried Harrison back until they could place him into the hands of the medics.

After a short stint in a military hospital, Harrison was back home with a Purple Heart, and a black-and-blue spirit. His wounded soul was out of sight, but the injury to his ear was not. Although no one would admit it, his visible injury certainly caused him to be denied some job opportunities. But besides that, his greatest difficulty in obtaining and maintaining employment was his invisible injury—his broken spirit. He tried drowning his guilt with liquor, but even his most patient and gracious employers were eventually forced to let him go. In less than two years after returning home, he had given up on society, and vice versa.

A small car rattled up behind the tavern, and Candy worked her way out of it to the back door. She saw Harold on the ground, slumped over on his knees, and called out, "Harold, Hun? You okay?" as she continued inside without waiting for a reply.

Harold snapped back from his memories, and tried to keep his head steady as he struggled back to his feet. He unlocked the bathroom door, and turned on the light. Inside, the floor and walls had been covered with ceramic tile, and were surprisingly clean. It was setup as a wet bath: one side contained a toilet with a bidet hose, and a small area with a handheld shower head. There was a large drain in the middle of the room, and all water that reached the floor courteously flowed into it. The other side contained a sink, a large mirror, and a hanging cabinet. Inside the cabinet, Harold kept his detergents, toiletries, a squeegee, and a duffle bag with clean clothes—or more accurately, *cleaned* clothes. About five feet from the ground there was a retractable laundry line that could be extended the full length of the room. Harold used this for hang-drying his clothes after hand-washing them in the sink. With access to this room and the other benefits of the tavern, Harold's essential needs were met. And compared to other homeless people, he thought himself fortunate.

After locking himself in, Harold showered, hand-washed last night's dumpster-wear, and hung them to dry. He washed his hat, and wrung out the water as best he could. But the only place he ever hung the hat to dry was on top of his wet head, and he was never seen without it. Once refreshed, he sprayed down and tidied up the room, donned the clothes from the duffle, and reset the cabinet. Something of his military training was still manifested in his care of these facilities. Other than the dripping laundry, it was as if he had never been there. He exited back into the morning sun, and locked the door behind him.

The washing of man and material made a considerable difference. Although he still looked impoverished, he no longer appeared or smelled repulsive. He could almost be described as handsome in a rugged and raggedy sort of way. He boldly walked inside the tavern, and found Candy unpacking boxes of liquor and restocking shelves.

For the sake of his headache, Harold spoke softly, "I need to use the phone."

"It's right here behind the counter, Hun! Go ahead."

"But I need to use the phone *in private*."

Candy stopped what she was doing, and glared back at him saying, "I've got work to do here!"

Harold slightly winced at the sound of her voice, but calmly replied, "Then let me use the office phone."

Candy's mouth dropped open in disgust. But realizing that she had no other option, she said, "Oh, alright! But don't take anything from the office, or it'll be your head!"

Harold muttered, "Believe me, I know."

Harold dialed, and the call was answered almost before it rang, but no one spoke. Harold began, "It's me, Harrison. I saw some red-headed guy in a black car last night taking pictures of the tavern. I'm sure it was an unmarked vehicle because the plates weren't standard issue. It was about nine o'clock. Yessir, I'm sorry I didn't call last night, but ... I wasn't really thinking, you understand. It wasn't until this morning that I remembered. I know. I'm sorry, sir. Okay, I'll tell her."

Harold walked out of the office, and as he walked by Candy he simply said, "Running yellow." And he left.

Kite hung up the phone, and immediately called G and T to come for an urgent meeting. Within thirty minutes, they were both present, and the urgency of Kite's call had made them both feel unusually nervous. Kite was sitting at his desk, and motioned for them to sit down. Kite began, "It seems that we may be under investigation, boys." And amidst their unsettled expressions, he explained the call he had received from Harold Harrison. "Of course, you know what this means?" Kite asked.

T replied, "We're running yellow, right?"

"Correct!" Kite replied, pleased by T's correctness.

G asked, "Sorry, Kite, but doesn't 'running yellow' mean 'running scared'?"

Kite's pleasure waned into disgust. He spoke sternly, "It means that we are running our operations at 'yellow alert,' you idiot! You and T are to take absolutely *no* new clients. As far as you are concerned, you are nothing more than bouncers at the tavern. And any unknown customers must be assumed to be undercover cops. Do you understand?!?"

G embarrassingly replied, "Yeah, I remember now."

Kite shouted, "Of course you remember *now*, you moron! I just told you!!!"

Attempting to regain his composure, Kite quietly replied, "We need to let things cool off for a while. Such a shame, too! Yesterday, I received both the down-payment from Mister Brighton, and a copy of the changes to Missus Brighton's will. I was planning on being somewhat richer by the end of this week. Now I'll have to wait a while, possibly even a few months."

T's brow had crinkled, and he asked, "Why don't you just find out who the cop is, and bump him off?"

Kite's face flushed with anger. He clenched his teeth for a moment before he said, "Because unlike the movies, we do not have a huge organization with unlimited resources. And an investigation into a slain officer who was already investigating the tavern would almost certainly uncover *you*. And once they've uncovered you, they would almost certainly uncover *me*! Did both of you pop idiot-pills for breakfast?!? The best tactic is to let things cool off. Investigators are on a payroll. And if there's no activity in their investigation, they'll eventually be forced by their superiors to move on to other things. Now go!"

Chapter Ten

It was nine o'clock on that same Tuesday morning that Joseph sat at his work desk, reading his computer screen. The cold pale green of the fluorescent lights above made the room feel like a giant freezer, completely empty except for Joseph sitting like a block of freezer-burned meat. His eyes were scowled in disgust as he attempted to fortify himself for the difficult task at hand. On his screen was the website of a flower delivery service where advertisements of fawning men and flirting women littered Joseph's eyes. The contradiction of selecting a surprise bouquet for his hated spouse had caused him to hesitate. Like the voice of a devil on his shoulder, he softly spoke to himself, "Outward appearance is crucial. This will help prevent suspicion. I must send her flowers today, although I'd prefer they were poisoned weeds!" With a few clicks of the mouse his choice was resolved, and his order placed. Then a fearful thought crossed his mind, and he whispered, "Oh no! Sending her flowers is easy enough, but how am I going to behave when I see her?!?"

Like the monsoon rains of the Sonoran desert, Lillian's morning had blown by in a flash. She had long forgotten the pleasant days of her youth and early adulthood when she actually felt joy in living. The days had become so cluttered with agony that she now believed any distraction to be a pleasure. But this folly was just one of the small foxes spoiling her heart, and certainly not the worst. Thus, immersing herself in work was her only relief, her only anesthesia against despair. Like so many others, she unwittingly exchanged a sickness of the heart for a sickness of the mind. She now sat at her desk, scrutinizing various production reports with such intensity that she didn't notice Joanna standing in her open doorway.

"You hungry?" Joanna asked.

Lillian's entire body convulsed in surprise, which made her knock her knees against the underside of the desk.

"Ow!" she exclaimed, and then grin-frowned with embarrassment.

Joanna couldn't prevent laughing throughout her apologies, "Oh, Lily! I'm so sorry! I thought you saw me standing here. It seems like I'm always startling you. It's not on purpose—really!"

Lillian rubbed her knee, and replied, "Yes, I am."

Joanna's concern for Lillian's shock now waned into confusion. "What?"

Lillian replied, "You asked if I'm hungry. Yes, I am."

Still chuckling, Joanna replied, "Oh, yeah! That's why I came. I figured since it's Friday, maybe we could order some Chinese delivery. They're right down the street, so it should get here quick. What'dya think?"

Lillian thought for a moment about her limp and browning salad sitting in the cooler on her office floor, then replied, "Sure. Why not?"

Just then, Lillian's desk phone beeped, and the receptionist, Sarah, began to speak. From the subtle inflections in her words, one could tell that Sarah was smiling ear-to-ear. There was also a childish excitement in her tone as she said, "Missus Brighton, you have a delivery. Would you like to come here, or should I escort the delivery guy to your office?"

Lillian looked toward Joanna with confusion, and said, "I'm not expecting any deliveries today."

Sarah quickly responded, "I didn't think so. But he's still here. May I escort him to your office, please?"

"Well, that depends on what it is."

"I'm not supposed to say, but I think you'd prefer to receive it in your office."

Lillian rolled her eyes, and complied, "Very well. Bring him here."

Within a minute, Sarah peeked around the door grinning like a politician on campaign, and said, "Close your eyes." Lillian scowled back in refusal, and Sarah huffed back, "Okay, fine! Be that way!"

Sarah stepped out of the doorway, and in walked a large bouquet of two dozen roses in a white ceramic vase with a rose motif. Half of the roses were pink, and the other half crimson, and the colorful accents of beautiful-but-lesser flowers supported the composition. Lillian seemed unaffected by the romantic notion of this gift, but the enthusiasm of Sarah and Joanna made up for her deficiency. Even the delivery man was obliged to take part in the festivities.

Joanna admired, "Aw! That's so sweet!"

Sarah sighed, "They're beautiful!"

The delivery man interrupted, "Excuse me?"

"What a lovely arrangement!"

"These must've cost a fortune!"

"Pardon me, miss?"

"Who are they from?"

"Is there a card?"

"Miss?!? Can I set these down somewhere?"

Sarah's attention was finally garnered, and she motioned to a clear spot on the desk. The vase hovered down and landed, revealing a stern-faced and unfeeling creature entirely contrary to the delicate rose petals and Baby Breath flowers. After a quick, "Sign here please," he was gone, and Sarah and Joanna resumed their admirations.

A card was perched in the middle of the assembly, on a small plastic pitchfork which seemed—to Lillian—as if it was offered from below by the devil himself. She quickly grabbed it, and her jaw clenched as she read the autograph.

"Who's it from, Lily?" the ladies pestered.

She cooly replied, "Satan."

Sarah and Joanna stood gaping in shock, and Lillian suddenly remembered her need for appearances. She smiled and chuckled, "I'm just kidding, ladies! They're from my husband. We had been having some tension at home, but I've really been trying to smooth things out. He must've taken notice, and he's sending a peace offering."

The ladies sighed in relief, and Sarah said, "You really gave me a jolt there for a minute!"

Lillian laughed, "Sorry about that! I suppose that was in bad taste. Ha ha! Thank you, Sarah! Oh, Joanna, can you please close my office door on your way out? Let me know when the food arrives. Thanks."

Joanna whispered back and smiled, "I'm so happy for you, Lily!"

Lillian smiled back until the door shut, then sat pondering and staring at the flowers. Then like a time-lapse of drying fruit, her face seemed to dry out, shrivel up, and turn moldy, and she reached for the phone. "Hello, can I speak with Charlie Parson, please? Hi, is this Charlie? This is Lillian Brighton. Yes, Joseph's wife. Sorry to call unannounced, but I'm planning a surprise dinner for my husband's birthday—a week from today—and I wanted to find out if you could help me by secretly inviting some of his work friends? You will? Oh, thank you! Can you give me your email so I can send the details? Okay, I'm ready to write it down."

After scratching down his response on a nearby paper, she replaced the handset, and continued planning to herself. "So, Joe, you give me years of hell and think that some flowers are going to cover it? I'll let you *think* they did, and put on a show by celebrating your birthday."

Chapter Eleven

Almost three weeks later on Friday morning, Moti sat in his jail cell like a weeping willow, drooping over his knees, staring at the ground. He thought to himself, "Twenty nights I've lost in here! How many more?!?" He thought of his future, how he might be sent to prison for a crime he didn't commit. And even if he was acquitted, how could he possibly continue his carpet cleaning business? The stain of accusation would never wash out of his reputation nor his own conscience. For it was his own conscience that tormented him more than the suspicions of the police. He remembered all too well his fall into drunken hatred. He remembered with sober clarity his desire for revenge. He remembered like a spotlight shining at midnight how the very designs he was trying to create had actually come to pass—Ross Boyd had in fact been killed. And although Moti knew that he was not the murderer, he still felt that he was somehow responsible. His voice had become deep and scratchy from disuse, and now sounded like that of someone who had risen too early after a late night. Yet he managed to croak out, "Ruined by *myself*. Always a loser."

Suddenly, like a juggler interrupting a funeral, Detective Clarke eagerly burst in, "Do not despair, Mister Martinez! Let's talk."

Officer Jacobs stepped out from behind Clarke, attempting to give Moti a comforting grin. But when Moti saw him, the shame of threatening Boyd and consequently being handcuffed by Jacobs that horrible day rushed back in. Moti's eyes closed, and his face fell into his palms as he lamented, "Oh, God! The police witness!"

Clarke laughed, and reassured him, "No, nothing like that, Mister Martinez," as he opened the cell. "Please stand up, and follow us. We'd just like to have a talk with you."

They shackled Moti as "standard procedure," led him out of the holding area, and eventually down a hall that would've been empty except for the occasional officer or legal worker passing by. There were a few doors evenly spaced on one side of the hall. Clarke opened the last door, and casually walked inside. Moti cautiously entered the room, looking this way and that, as if expecting someone or something to jump out and grab him. Officer Jacobs gently nudged Moti forward until he could close the door behind them, and then stood like a sentinel before it.

The room was completely empty except for a small table in the middle, and two chairs facing each other on opposite sides of the table. There were also two cameras in opposite corners of the ceiling, and on either side of the room, one facing each chair at an angle. Clarke walked around the table, sat down, and pulled a notebook out of his briefcase. Moti realized that this was an interrogation room, and felt his legs and hands began to quiver with anxiety. Clarke looked at Moti, motioned to the empty chair and said, "Please have a seat." Moti quickly sat down in fear that he might faint.

Clarke turned to Jacobs and asked, "Is the observation area secure?" Jacobs gave a quick nod in the affirmative, and Clarke turned back to Moti who was now looking wide-eyed and catatonic.

"Breathe, Mister Martinez!" Clarke demanded. "We're not here to interrogate you. We're here to help you."

Moti blinked, and after three or four deliberately deep breaths, his color began to return. "Why'd you bring me here?" he asked.

"You stumbled into the middle of a dark web of deception and crime," Clarke began, "and I have finally started to obtain what I need to bring the culprits to justice."

Moti bumbled, "That doesn't include *me*, right? I mean, you know *I* ain't a culprit! Right?!?"

Clarke grinned back, "That's correct. *I* do not believe you are the culprit. However, the evidence against you is quite compelling in the eyes of the law. So I need to build my case against those who I believe to be the *real* culprits before I can get you released. That is why I brought you here. I believe that the person called 'Kite' is the leader of a small but highly organized gang, and *you* are the only person I know who has actually seen and spoken with him. I need you to tell me every little detail from that encounter, no matter how insignificant it might seem. Can you do that? I already know about the bar—the Hemlock Tavern. But tell me whatever else you can remember of the man himself."

Moti, attempting to calm himself, replied, "Well, I was pretty wasted, but I'll tell you what I know. He called himself 'Kite,' *like the bird of prey*," Moti emphasized knowingly. "His face looked to be about forty, with short hair, like an army guy. And, man did he look *bad*!"

Clarke interrupted, "What do you mean, 'bad'? He looked *evil*, somehow?"

Moti continued, "Naw, I mean *baaaad*! Like he was *super-cut* for his age! His arms were *buff*, and even his legs looked solid! I bet he could fight! Even his *boys* seemed to be afraid of him, and they looked like *juicers*! I mean, he's one tough looking dude."

Clarke, too busy making notes to look up said, "Very good. Please continue."

Moti was now feeling so comfortable, he seemed to forget that he was in the presence of police officers. He slouched in his chair, and said, "That's about it. I mean, he was asking for twenty grand to knock people off— he kept calling them 'The Package'—but when I told him I didn't have any money, he got all upset and had me taken back to the bar."

Clarke perked up, "Before I forget, *where* did you meet him? What kind of place was it?"

Moti leaned forward, "That's one of the things I thought was weird. We were actually inside a bedroom in a *house*. It was setup like an office, but I'm sure it was just a regular bedroom. And I'm pretty sure it was a newer house, too. Now that I think about it, I remember the carpet was really nice and modern—couldn't have been more than three or four years old."

Clarke interjected, "Do you remember how long it took to drive back to the bar?"

Moti squinted in thought, "I'm really not sure. I think I dozed off on the way there. And all the way back my head was hurting so bad I couldn't think!"

Clarke scratched and dotted his last note, and said, "Mister Martinez, you have been of material assistance. I'm going to have to return you to your cell now. But do not lose heart! I'm going to use the info I got from you today to try to locate and arrest this guy before anyone else gets hurt."

Then Moti's sadness returned, and he asked, "What about my stuff? I mean, my apartment?"

"Ah, yes!" Clarke replied. "There's good news and bad news in that. I spoke with your landlady, and she's preparing to clear out your apartment if the rent isn't paid in two weeks." Moti gasped as Clarke continued, "*However*, since I feel somewhat responsible for you being in here, I have personally arranged for movers to put your things into storage if you're not out in time. I'm sorry, but that's the best I could do."

Although this wasn't exactly what Moti had hoped, Clarke's gesture of kindness actually touched him deeply, and his eyes watered up as he said, "That means a lot to me, Detective Clarke. Thank you."

Clarke's face quickly became stern, and he warned Moti, "Now remember this, Moti—er, Mister Martinez: do *not* speak of 'Kite' or anything else to *anyone* other than myself or Officer Jacobs. Do you understand?"

Moti agreed, "Sure, I understand. But it's just my luck that the only two cops who ever arrested me are now the only two I'm supposed to *trust*!"

Chapter Twelve

Within two miles from the police station where Moti was being held stood the Jizo Shelter for Women and Children. This beautiful Saturday's dawn offered hope to this suffering community, driving away the darkness with its lovely amber light. The several buildings comprising the shelter had originally been constructed about forty years earlier as a small apartment complex of thirty six units. With a centrally located recreation room, the apartments had boasted a ping-pong table, billiards, and free family films every month. For a fortunate three-dozen families in those decades gone by, leases were secured in this idyllic community which seemed to have been born as a microcosm of the notions of Sir Thomas More. But over the years, the natural decay of greed, apathy, and entropy had taken their toll upon this once envied residence. And within two decades of its construction, it had become a notorious ghetto, populated only by the criminal class or those too impoverished to live elsewhere. After being central to some scandalous lawsuits, the property lay vacant several years until even the "For Sale" signs began to look dilapidated. Three years ago, however, the property had been purchased by a Trust, and was quickly converted into the charity that stood today— where an unfortunate few now found temporary residence when trying to escape abuse. The Trustee was said to be a true philanthropist—a man who *really cared*, and operated two more similar compounds around town. Every month, he would pay one visit to each shelter when he would to try to impart some character virtues into the poor children living there. Sometimes he would read them stories, or host a physical education class, or teach them basic self-defense moves, or play games with them in the refurbished recreation center. For the children, those days were like Christmas, and that man was nothing less than Santa Claus.

Today's Christmas was just ending. The heroic Santa was waving goodbye to the fawning children as he walked out of the cast-iron gate which was immediately shut and—bzzzztt!—electronically locked for their safety. As he approached his white S.U.V., he noticed a shabby but clean figure waiting by the driver's side door. It was the resident drunk of the Hemlock Tavern, Harold Harrison. Harrison looked unsettled, and kept casting nervous glances this-way-and-that. The closer Santa got to the vehicle, the more his jovial manner and countenance changed into his stern and ruthless alter ego, Kite.

Kite's displeasure could not be hidden as he spoke, "What are you doing here, Harrison? This had better be serious."

Harrison, still jumpy with nervous energy, replied, "Believe me, sir, I wouldn't have come if not. And I was afraid to call."

"Afraid of what?!?" Kite demanded.

"Surveillance, sir. We need to talk."

Kite studied his face and manner, and somehow a single drop of Harrison's lake of sincerity and agitation transferred to himself, and he gently replied, "Alright. Get in."

As they started to leave, Harrison looked toward the shelter where one or two children stood inside the fence waving as Kite drove away. Harrison's thoughts began to escape as he said, "I realize you need to channel your money somehow, but I don't understand why you'd use a *charity* to do it."

Kite glanced over, and his eyes betrayed a genuine tenderness as he explained, "I don't *use* the charity, Harrison. I operate it for the sake of the kids. Those kids are *innocent. They* haven't done anything wrong, but they've been wronged nonetheless." Kite's voice began to betray restrained rage as he continued, "And what 'help' does the *government* give? Instead of *helping* the moms, they sometimes *punish* them! They blame the *mother* for not raising their child in a safe environment! But is it *mom's* fault if the creep she's living with is abusive? No! And where can she go to get away? As far as she knows, nowhere! So someone calls in the government, and their agent has a drumhead trial at the front door declaring, 'This environment isn't *safe* for little Olly!' So they step in, take away the little boy, and put him in foster home after foster home. And then that poor kid learns how evil people can be. The *adults* take advantage and hurt that innocent boy until he can't even remember what 'innocent' means! And why is that boy suffering through all of this? Because the *government* wanted him in a 'safe environment'!" Kite's deep fury could be heard even though he had never shouted. Then he calmly said, "*That* is why I operate the charity, Harrison. Because *I* know better than they do what a safe environment really is, and what it *isn't*. *I* know how to protect kids without taking them from their moms, unlike the government's 'child protectors,' who seem to enjoy causing more harm than good. So I play the government like the fools they are, I manipulate the *system*, and I get them to give me money to protect the innocent while I simultaneously punish the guilty."

The rest of the drive, neither of the men spoke, but sat like ancient trees, leaning under the weight of their burdensome limbs.

They arrived at Kite's home and base of operations, and Kite ushered Harrison into his meeting room. They both sat, facing each other across the desk, and Harrison knew well enough to wait for Kite to begin. Kite sat upright, and with analytical keenness focused his attention on Harrison.

Then he spoke, "Alright, Harrison. You said you were afraid, and we needed to talk. So talk."

Harrison sat like a man whose chair was made of ice, and began to explain, "Remember about three weeks ago, the cop I told you about?" Kite didn't move, but continued to intently listen and observe. Harrison continued, "He was the red-headed guy in the black car. Well he was back at the tavern, very late last night. I was inside, over in the corner, when he walked in wearing plain clothes. He stepped up to the bar, ordered a beer, and went and sat down off to the side, watching and listening to everyone. I noticed that, although he kept lifting the glass to his mouth, he wasn't really drinking anything 'cause the beer never went down in the glass. Then, before I could do anything, he had looked me right in the eyes, got up from his seat, and walked over and sat down at my table! And he started probing me for information, but very subtly."

Kite tensed up, and interjected, "What sort of information? What did you tell him?!?"

"Nothing! I mean, I told him nothing *important*. He was mostly interested in *me*, which I thought was weird. Like, he asked, 'How often do you come to this tavern?' And, 'Do you have any other bars you'd recommend?' Stuff like that. After a few minutes, he looked at my ear, and said, 'That's some scar you've got there. I'll bet there's a heck of a story in it!' I told him that it was a combat injury from my stint in the army. He asked where I had fought, and I told him I didn't like to talk about it. He pressed me, so I ended up telling him a little about Kuwait, and how I had been pulled from the field by my sergeant and another private. He said, 'So you were a private, too?' Trying to be cordial, I saluted him and said, 'Private Harold Harrison, reporting for duty, sir!' He chuckled at first, but then he quieted his voice, and started whispering about other people in the tavern, probably trying to see if I knew any of them. But since I didn't, he got up to leave. I tried asking him for *his* name, and he leaned over, face to face, and whispered, 'I'm nobody. Just a guy looking to fly a *kite*.' My eyes and mouth must've both opened wide, and he seemed to be able to look into my mind through my eyes! It seemed like he could see a picture of *you* there in my reaction! He laughed out loud without taking his eyes off of mine, and then walked out of the tavern smiling. Ever since, I've been feeling paranoid again, like my breakdown after the war! I feel like I'm being watched all the time, like I'm about to be attacked from behind!"

At the moment, Kite's concern for Harrison was somewhat less than his concern for himself. For the first time, he was hearing a truly unsettling report, and it made Kite feel like he might be vulnerable. He had nerves of steel when he was playing the predator, but no tolerance for being the prey. He collected himself, folded his hands calmly, and spoke deliberately, "Please be quiet for a moment. I need to think." After two or three minutes of sitting and staring through his hands, Kite leaned back confidently, put his hands behind his head, and said, "Well, it seems obvious enough that they're on to the tavern, so I suppose I will have to close it and open a new one elsewhere. I may even have to change my alias. It was certainly that carpet-cleaning rat who said something, so I'll send Wilkes a message to deal with him as soon as possible. But don't worry, Harrison. The government might've dumped you after the war, but *I* won't. I'll make sure you're provided for, no matter what happens."

Harrison's answer started like a reflex, "Thanks, Sarge. Er, sorry. I meant, *Kite*. Thanks, Kite." Then Harrison leaned forward, and his eyes seemed to be pleading as he asked, "Kite? Why not get out of this now? I mean, things have changed. You've got other options now—*legitimate* income. And it's starting to get too risky. I don't mind being your eyes-and-ears in the field. And I'm grateful for all the help you've given me. But I'm starting to think that maybe I don't want to spend the rest of my life like this—being the town *drunk*, and waking up in dumpsters. I want to get *clean*, get a job— try to make it on my *own* again. I certainly don't want to wake up behind bars."

Kite looked at him with an almost fatherly compassion, and told him, "Harrison, I am sincerely happy to hear that you're wanting to better yourself. And I promise you that I would never hinder you, or do anything to hurt your efforts to succeed in life. I didn't abandon you on the battlefield—like the government did after you returned. However, as for *me*, I do not think I can ever go back to a normal civilian life. My steps are already laid down in stone, and I am resolved to be the man that *they* made me to be. As a young man, I went to the government to try to *give* myself to help the oppressed people of the world, and the government trained me to be a soldier—to be a *killer*. And so I gave myself to be the *best* killer I could be, and accelerated to the rank of sergeant. When I returned from the war, did the government thank me? Did they give me a hero's welcome? Did they even give me a *job*?!? No! They abandoned me! They abandoned *all* of us, Harrison! I even tried to get on the police force, an occupation where my skills would've truly been useful, but they rattled off some nonsense about my 'psychological profile,' and rejected me offhandedly! The very government that trained me to be a *killer* rejected me for being a *killer*! So I *must* be what I was made to be, and I am resolved to be the *best*." Kite's face now looked forbidding and cold, with a morbid frown and tight lips, like someone embalmed and lying in a coffin.

Harrison nodded in affirmation and gratitude, but secretly thought to himself, "I thought *I* was the only one who was still bleeding on the inside, but Sarge's wounds are far worse than mine! And when he speaks —my God!—I feel as if my wounds are being ripped back open all over again! If I'm ever going to find healing, I must get out of this—now!!!"

Chapter Thirteen

On that same Saturday, Joseph and Lillian were both at home, yet no where near each other. Joseph was preparing to go golfing, and Lillian was apparently sleeping in. The past three weeks had begun as one bizarre charade followed by another, which we must now recount.

That first day, when Joseph sent the large floral bouquet to Lillian's workplace, he was unsure if he would be able to disguise his hatred at home that night. As it turned out, he didn't even have to try. When Lillian returned home, Joseph may as well have been invisible. She never acknowledged his presence with either glance or word, but behaved as though she was entirely alone in the house. She prepared her own dinner, spent some time engrossed in her mobile tablet and headphones—whether reading the news, or watching videos, Joseph wasn't certain and didn't care enough to ask. He was slouched in his recliner, watching nothing in particular on television, and numb to the world around him. It was almost two hours later when he turned off the T.V. and noticed that the common area of the house was vacant and silent. Lillian, as quiet as a cat, had apparently gone to bed without any ado. For the past few days, Joseph had been sleeping in the spare room, so he retired, relieved that the flowers had not required any further acting on his part—especially in private.

Three days later, on Friday, Joseph was busy at work examining a spreadsheet of a departmental budget when Alan's head popped around the door. With eyebrows raised and smile beaming, Alan blurted, "Happy birthday!"

Joseph's face turned toward Alan, but his thoughts were obviously still lost in the numbers on his computer screen as he muttered, "What was that? Birthday? Whose birthday is it?"

"It's *your* birthday, you goof! Did you seriously forget?!?"

Joseph peered in confusion, and looked at the calendar on his wall as he said, "I guess I did. My mind has been elsewhere."

Alan shook his head in disbelief, and snickered as he said, "Listen, Charlie and I want to buy you dinner after work—our treat." Joseph opened his mouth to protest as Alan interrupted, "You cannot say no because we've already made reservations at *Le Haute Saveur* under *your* name, and we've requested a special bottle of *aged* wine—like *you*!" And like a grinning phantom, Alan disappeared back into the cube farm outside Joseph's office.

After work, Joseph arrived at the restaurant, and was escorted to his table. It was a much larger table and group than he had expected. As his eyes adapted to the dim light of the restaurant's *ambiance*, he was just starting to make out the guests in his party. There was Charlie and his wife, Jan—"What's *she* doing here?" Joseph wondered. And there was Ralph and his wife, Becky, as well. "Hmmm, that's also odd," Joseph thought, but continued to work his way around the other tables. Alan made eye-contact with Joseph, and patting the empty chair at his left, motioned for Joseph to sit. Next to the chair sat a woman facing the other way. As she turned around to greet Joseph—*thwack!*—her face struck like a rock to the head. It was his dearly hated Lillian! She sat there smiling as if they were on the best of terms. In less than one second, Joseph's face contorted with a series of emotions including shock, disdain, fury, fear, self-composure, and pretense. As he sat down, he forced a half-hearted smile, and everyone gave a discombobulated whisper-shout of "Surprise!"

For the rest of the night, Joseph was slightly turned to the right, away from Lillian, seemingly interested in his conversation with his coworkers. And Lillian likewise turned to the left, engaged in chitchat with the other ladies. Despite Joseph and Lillian's discomfort with each other, they actually did enjoy themselves at the dinner party—albeit separately. Lillian was the first to excuse herself, as she said, in order to pay the tab. And although Joseph left the restaurant only ten minutes later, by the time he got home, Lillian had already closed the master bedroom door, and probably barricaded it, as well. Down the hall, Joseph could clearly hear the shower in the master bathroom running, but unaffectedly went to bed in the other room where, as he thought, he could have peace and quiet.

Joseph was not an oversleeper, but Sunday morning it was after nine o'clock when he finally emerged. The master bedroom door was open, and as Joseph peeked in he noticed that Lillian's exercise shoes were missing, so he assumed she had gone to the gym. He fuddled his way to the coffee pot, then after obtaining the steaming reward of his patience, carefully sat down at his computer, all the while carefully sipping the aromatic cup. Friday's dinner had left him feeling one-upped by Lillian, and that would not do. He began searching online, and found a company that would deliver fancy chocolates in romantic packaging. He ordered delivery at Lillian's workplace, once again scheduled for the mid-morning of tomorrow, "the perfect distraction to everyone's Monday blues," he thought.

The next day, Joseph's strategy seemed to be working perfectly as Lillian could not discourage the other ladies at work from admiring the red-laced chocolate box and the hoopla made by its arrival. Lillian was not flattered, but was contrariwise put on the defensive. Like a border dispute between two countries, the next two weeks were filled with tit-for-tat gifts, always delivered in the presence of friends at work. Lillian counterattacked by sending Joseph a singing telegram, and Joseph responded with a fruitcake. Next Lillian sent Joseph and his coworkers an hors d'oeuvre tray, and Joseph followed up with gourmet cookies. Eventually, Lillian retaliated by sending a "Just Because" cake addressed to Joseph, with instructions that it was to be shared with everyone. Food in the workplace draws people out of their cubicles as quickly as the Pied Piper lured away the children of Hamelin. Thus, when the rumor of a cake rushed through the area, many people congregated near the delivery man, and followed him joyfully as he pranced to the break room. Lillian also included the following poem to be read aloud by the delivery person:

There's nothing that can beat,
The sweet as sweet as sweets,
And such a welcome treat,
Must be shared by those in reach,
But sweetened cocoa in a vat,
Tends to make the eater fat,
And I'd rather give back that,
Than have to work it off.

Everyone was amused, not only by Lillian's stylish wit, but all the more because she had included them as recipients of her giving. As this treat was being divided among the vultures, Joseph interpreted the message of Lillian's verse based upon her desire for fitness—she was not impressed by his gifts of fattening foods. He was going to have to feign sensitivity to her preferences in order for his act to continue to be believable.

Joseph was forced to take some time to think about Lillian's likes and dislikes. These were memories he had not visited for many years, and which he was disturbed to explore. Thinking of what she liked meant thinking of her being happy. When she had been happy, Joseph had been happy. And now those memories not only interfered with his hatred, but provoked his sense of the good times that had been lost. Then—ding!—the lightbulb appeared above his head as he remembered something. Lillian used to have a near-obsession for sliced cucumbers sprinkled with mild chili powder, salt, and a touch of lime juice. Although he hadn't seen her eat them in a few years, he knew that a gift like that would almost certainly require an explanation to her coworkers. It would be the perfect ploy! But he knew he would not be able to find a delivery service for such a customized request. He would have to make the gift, and perform the delivery himself.

During his lunchtime, Joseph ran to the grocery store, and picked up the items necessary for his current scheme. He couldn't risk preparing this at home, so he returned to work, and placed the groceries in the break room refrigerator. The next day was Friday, and Joseph decided he would take a long lunch to finish preparing and delivering the spiced cucumbers. In the break room, he cleaned a portion of the counter, and set up shop for his culinary project. He washed and sliced the cucumbers, and sprinkled the chili powder carefully, so as to preserve the look of the thing. He had purchased a disposable party tray which he sprinkled with lime juice before aesthetically arranging the chili-spangled slices the best he could. Throughout the time he was working, several people came and went, looking over his shoulder, and asking what he was doing. He would simply say, "It's a gift for my wife," and most of them would wistfully commend his efforts. After he covered the entire platter with plastic and gift wrap, he completed the work by embellishing it with a bow. For a brief moment, as he beheld the gift, Joseph actually felt proud of himself, and smiled with that special pleasure that is only felt by those who give for the sake of giving. Then he remembered the sinister drama that he was trying to maintain, and quickly resolved to deliver the package without delay.

Lillian had already eaten when Sarah once again began beeping in on the intercom, and excitedly alerting her of another romantic delivery. Lillian sighed as she waited for the sideshow to begin. She wasn't sure if she felt relief or disappointment when Sarah walked in by herself, holding the rather lackluster gift platter that was obviously not crafted by a professional.

"Where's the delivery guy?" Lillian asked, trying not to sound let down.

Sarah said, "There wasn't a delivery guy this time. Your husband dropped this off himself. What a sweetheart!"

Lillian couldn't believe her ears. "Are you sure?!?" she exclaimed.

"Absolutely certain," Sarah said as she placed the platter on Lillian's desk. "And he told me to make sure I get you to explain it to me, whatever that means. Gotta run!" Just then, the main line began to ring, and Sarah hurried back to her desk.

Lillian quickly peeled open the wrapping paper, and saw the snacks inside. Her throat began to involuntarily shake as she struggled to hold back a fit of uncontrollable sobbing. She swiftly got up to shut and lock her office door, then she fell back into her chair and began weeping. Joseph was correct in remembering that this would be a significant gift for Lillian, but he did not understood how or why it would be felt so deeply.

Although Lillian had grieved, the pain of her father's death was never too far removed. Her mother had passed away when she was too young to remember, and her father became one of those remarkable people who make a child feel like one parent is enough. He was all she had ever known or needed. And losing him had left an emptiness in her heart that no one, not even Joseph, had tried to fill.

One of the things that made Lillian's father special was that he always attached meaning to ordinary things and experiences. One such thing was sliced cucumbers with chili powder, salt, and lime juice. Lillian's fondest early memories included her being with her father in the kitchen, preparing this snack together.

Lillian remembered herself as a young girl, and her father cutting a slice of cucumber. Without adding any chili, salt, or lime juice, he handed it to her and asked, "How do you like the taste of plain cucumber, Lily?"

Lily munched the slice, crumpled her nose, and spoke through her chewing, "It's not very good."

Then her father put just a little of the chili powder on her finger, and said, "Now taste that by itself?"

Lily licked the powder, and frowned, "That's a little spicy, but not good at all."

Her father put some lime juice in her little hand, and smiling said, "Now try that by itself."

As she licked the juice, her mouth tightened from the tartness and she said, "Ew!"

Finally, her father sliced another cucumber, and added to it all the spices: the chili powder, salt, and a drop or two of lime juice, then asked, "Try this one with everything," and smiled as he handed it to her.

Lily popped it in her mouth, and her eyes brightened as she said, "That's my favorite!"

Her father told her, "Remember this Lily. All people are like cucumbers and spices. We're not very good when we're alone, but when we're close with someone else, we can be very good together."

His words so long ago now stuck like goads into her embittered heart. She felt ashamed of her inner self. The years of marital conflict had made her so adept at identifying the faults in her husband that she had become completely blinded to the faults in herself. And now, these fond memories of a man whom she adored —and adored her—shone forth the hideous reflection of what she had allowed herself to become. She whispered his words to herself, "good *together*," and the pain of her hatred flushed her face, and once again she broke down. The contradiction of these words compared to her own marriage—how could they be resolved? Was her father-hero a man of deep wisdom, or was he just an idealistic fool? She could not tolerate such ill-thoughts against this beloved man, and she began to ponder. Her eyes and head bowed down, and half of her mouth smirked as she remembered softly, "when we're *close*." Her frown returned, and she wept out, "We're *not* close, Joe!" And she sat there shedding tears for the utter failure of recent years.

Joseph worked later than usual on that Friday afternoon. Although his position allowed him to leave when he wanted, he was in the middle of one of those analytical problems that are more difficult to start in the middle than to work to the end. After more than an hour, he was finally able to finish the task and leave the office. He stopped for a quick bite, and returned home resolved to kick off the shoes, and pay what remaining attention he had to the shining box in the living room. That area of the house was certainly misnamed the *living room*, as it would have been more appropriately called the *dying room*. Most of what happened in this room was certainly opposite of living, and it neither promoted nor supported life.

As Joseph sat like a rag doll, sprawled in the recliner, Lillian approached unnoticed from the master bedroom down the hall. Silhouetted from behind by the hall lights, she leaned against the wall with her arms gently crossed as if to protect herself from a gust of wind. She momentarily glanced at the activity on the screen before speaking just loud enough to be heard, "Thank you for the gift today."

Joseph looked over like a man awoken from sleep, and cooly replied, "Huh?"

Lillian slightly sniffled, and her voice sounded like she had a cold, or had been crying. She repeated, "The gift today. Thank you."

Joseph slowly turned back to the television, and said with duplicity, "It was nothing," as he secretly smirked in self-gratification.

Lillian regained her stance, and replied with a sincerity that shattered Joseph's cynicism, "Well, it was something to *me*, and I wanted to thank you for it," and she softly walked back to the bedroom and carefully closed the door.

Joseph continued to watch the television, but his thoughts seemed to dwell upon Lillian. Her behavior contradicted his beliefs about her, and his mind began to analyze each word, tone, and inflection in her speech, trying to reconcile the difference. His hateful instincts attempted to dismiss this as a manipulative ruse, a calculated tactic of warfare, a military push to gain ground. But there was nothing aggressive nor even defensive in her words or manner that he could detect. Indeed, he was baffled. For the first time in years, she seemed to be vulnerable. He turned off the T.V., and went to his bed in the spare room where he lay in thought, staring at the ceiling until he drifted to sleep.

The next morning, Joseph awoke and began to enthusiastically get ready to join Alan for a full round of golf, with a tee time just after ten o'clock—about the same time when Kite and Harrison were leaving the charitable compound. And that brings us back to where we left off.

As Joseph was getting ready, he noticed that the master bedroom door was still shut, and all was silent within. He couldn't help feeling a natural concern—or perhaps just curiosity—but he shrugged it off and headed out to his game.

It was after three o'clock when Joseph returned home. His putting had noticeably improved, and this had him in good spirits. He was opening the door, and starting to call out Lillian's name to share his success when he remembered that he was supposed to be angry and aloof. But when he thought of her gratitude the night before, he began to feel complex emotions. He didn't think about what he was feeling, or he might have described it as being angry for being angry. Or perhaps feeling sorry for not feeling sorry. However designated, it was an emotion that was introspective and self-judging. It was Joseph judging Joseph, something that had not happened in a long time. And all of these complexities were shrouded in common loneliness—for he had no one to share his life and experiences.

With all of these feelings weighing on his heart, his eyes and head became downcast as he subconsciously moseyed down the hall toward the master bedroom, toward Lillian. The door was still shut, and all seemed as still as a tomb. Joseph quietly and slowly opened the door just enough to peek in. He was astounded to see that Lillian was still in bed—at half-past three! But something in the position of her body seemed unnatural, so he opened the door and gently called out, "Lily?" He saw a very subtle movement of the bedcovers, but she didn't answer. Joseph walked in, around to Lillian's side of the bed, and while gently touching her shoulder said, "Lily, are you okay?"

Lillian was in a daze, and as Joseph looked closer at her face he could see at once by the dark areas around her eyes that she was not well. He shook her shoulder a little more firmly, and called out again, a little louder, "Lily? Lily? Can you hear me?"

Lillian was unresponsive, and Joseph began to feel instincts of panic. He quickly called the emergency number, and then futilely tried again to wake her. Her forehead was grotesquely hot to the touch, so Joseph got a cool wet washcloth, and applied it to her forehead until the paramedics arrived. Joseph led them into the bedroom, and stood out of the way, watching as they worked. Lillian's pajamas were cut off, and Joseph began feeling flushed by her lying there before these strangers with her modesty exposed. Who were these men, anyway? Although he was desperate for their help, they were in his *bedroom*, handling his wife like a baker with a pile of dough. Joseph spontaneously spoke, however faintly, "Be careful. Easy now." They seemed to not hear him as they were intent upon their work. In very few minutes, they had checked Lillian's vital signs, connected an I.V. to her hand, inserted an oxygen tube—a *nasal cannula*—in her nostrils, placed a draw sheet under her body, and hoisted her onto a gurney. After securing the gurney straps around her body, they wheeled her out of the house and into the ambulance. Joseph was too overwhelmed with the feelings of emergency to notice his neighbors peering out of windows, and whispering to each other in their homes.

Several hours later, as Joseph sat in the I.C.U. waiting lounge, a nurse entered and called out for Mister Brighton. Joseph was led down the hall into Lillian's room where a doctor stood reviewing her charts. He spoke, "Mister Brighton? Doctor Deiter. Please sit down," and Joseph complied.

He continued, "Your wife's condition is quite serious. When she arrived, her fever was one hundred and five degrees. We are force-feeding her liquids intravenously, but her fever …"

Although Joseph's eyes remained on the doctor, his mind began to be engulfed with the sights, sounds, and smells around him. Smells of antiseptics, disinfectants, medicinal creams, and rubbing alcohol all mixed with the subtle stench of sickly and unwashed bodies. The rhythmic beeps, pops, and whooshes of medical monitors and breathing machines became a morbid orchestra performing that last composition heard by so many people this side of eternity. The nauseous green hue of the hospital lights seemed to mock the vibrant and lively green of healthy plants and forests. The doctor's voice occasionally cut through, like a shout across distant mountain peaks, and Joseph would nod as if he understood. In fact, all he caught was that Lillian had a dangerously high fever, apparently viral in nature, and her own immune system would need to fight it off.

Doctor Deiter paused for a moment, and as he looked Joseph straight in the eyes, Joseph's thoughts were snapped back to attention. The doctor calmly said, "Also, Mister Brighton, I feel I must prepare you—if your wife does not improve within the next twenty four hours, we could lose her."

It was almost midnight when a taxi dropped Joseph in front of his house and drove off. Joseph stood at the curb, and turned facing the house. Ordinarily, the front door light would be lighting the entrance, but since he had left hurriedly, and somewhat in a state of shock, and with daylight to spare, Joseph had forgotten to turn it on. He noticed how much he and the house were alike: both utterly empty and completely filled with darkness.

He sauntered up the path—or rather stumbled— unlocked the door, and pushed it open without entering. Pausing at the threshold, he stared into the desolate house, pondering the past and present. Questions. All he could think were questions. The past which used to seem so linear and orderly now seemed to be a conglomerate of disparate and chaotic events that brought him here, to this moment, standing on this threshold, looking into a dark house.

134

He thought to himself, sometimes speaking aloud, "Why do I feel so empty? Why is this house so empty? Shouldn't there be kids here? I like kids. Why don't we have any kids? I remember Lily from long ago. I used to love her. Why do I hate her now? *Do* I really hate her? I'm worried about her. She might die. I don't want her to die. But I *did* want her to die, didn't I? This is what I wanted, isn't it? Is it possible, could this be *my* fault? Nonsense! I didn't make her sick! Or did I? Did *I* cause a sickness in her *soul* that has maybe moved into her *body*? Bah! That is more than I can know. But what about the man that I have become? What about the sickness in *my* soul? Who's to blame for *me*, the evil creature that I am today? Surely, *I* am *my* own fault! My God, what have I become?!?"

And for the first time in twenty years, Joseph fell to his knees, right there in the doorway, wailing in his misery.

Chapter Fourteen

Monday morning, Clarke wanted to meet with Jacobs away from the police station to discuss his progress and weekend discoveries. Despite the stereotypical donut-eating cops of television, these men were actually more temperate than their caricatures. They met for breakfast in a small homey restaurant where the youngest waitress could've been their mother, and the next youngest could've been hers. Clarke ordered oatmeal with raisins and nuts, and a side of whole grain toast. Jacobs ordered the "Farm Breakfast" which included three over-medium eggs, sausage links, hash browns, and toast. This place had impressive coffee, and the men usually enjoyed several cups with their meals.

After the waitress had taken their orders and hobbled away, Jacobs waited a minute for Clarke to begin. The detective was visibly distracted by his own thoughts, and stared at his coffee as if he was expecting something to jump out of his cup. Jacobs spoke, "So, how goes the case?"

Clarke looked up, and grinned, "Well done, Jacobs. Very subtle."

"Well, if I didn't say something soon, you'd have burned a hole through that cup the way you were staring at it."

Clarke chuckled, "Yeah, you're right. I suppose it's obvious that I'm concerned. That is to say, there's good news and bad news."

Jacobs interjected, "With you, there always is!"

Clarke continued, "Well, in a nutshell: the good news is that I think I've discovered who this man Kite is, and the bad news is that I don't have any tangible evidence to arrest him. Let me review everything up to this point, if not for your sake, for my own. Perhaps I've overlooked something that will occur to one of us. Do not withhold any ideas, nor assume that I've already had them. We *must* find a way to stop this villain, hopefully before anyone else suffers at his hand."

Jacobs astutely listened as Clarke proceeded to explain, "You remember Friday morning, when we spoke to Mister Martinez. I had already received the DNA results of that hair I found in your initial report on Martinez. As you know, it belonged to Officer Wilkes, and he *never* had a reason to be in that file. Fortunately, Wilkes had to submit DNA samples during his time in the military, as well as when he joined the force. So the lab was able to find a match a little quicker than usual, and their opinion was that the match was a ninety-six percent certainty. I knew that Wilkes couldn't be Kite himself because I verified that he was on duty the night that Martinez met with Kite. But I also verified that he was actually *in the station* at that time, and this supported my theory that he was the mole I was looking for. The problem I had to solve was how to identify who he was working for—the man called Kite. I couldn't subpoena his phone records based upon a single hair in a case file, especially since he's an officer working out of the same station. And Wilkes' online presence was virtually nonexistent: I could find no social media accounts to help identify his contacts. So I decided to interview Moti for clues—I mean Mister Martinez."

Jacobs smiled, "You like him. So do I."

Clarke grinned back, but his grin dissolved into a desperate agitation as he said, "Yes, I like him. But what's worse is that I *know* he's innocent, and he's in jail because *I* arrested him! And if he goes to trial, I'm not sure I can prevent him from going to prison! For the first time in my career, I think my self-righteousness might have made *me* the criminal!!!"

Jacobs tried to encourage him, "Clarke, *you* are not the criminal. *Kite* is. And *Wilkes* is. We've just got to figure out how to prove that, and Martinez will be free. And we *will* figure it out, so don't worry. Now tell me what else happened."

Clarke sighed, "Thanks, Jacob. You're right, of course. In fact, what I'm about to tell you should've comforted me before I spoke it. Anyway, let me go on.

"When I asked Moti to describe Kite, he mentioned something that interested me, that Kite's hair seemed to be a military cut. After the interview, I decided to research Wilkes' military records, and *that* is where I found him! Kite, I mean.

"Wilkes was a member of a squad of eight men that fought in Kuwait and Iraq during *Desert Storm*. Of the seven other men, three of them had been killed in action. And of the remaining four, I discovered that *two* of them were living here in town: Oliver Gunther, who was sergeant over the squad, and Harold Harrison, another private who was discharged with a Purple Heart —had the top of his ear shot off.

"I searched for these men in police records, and found something on Harrison. Last year, a few calls had come in about a body lying on a bench at a bus stop, and most thought he was dead. The responding officers discovered it was actually a passed-out drunk, none other than Mister Harold Harrison. There was no reason to arrest him, so they just sent him on his way. Fortunately, one of the officers filed a report.

"I didn't find anything on Oliver Gunther, so I decided to search for him in public records. I discovered that he is chairman of a trust that owns and operates three charity compounds for women and children, and also a single-family residence not far from the Hemlock Tavern. I verified that the only mail going to that address is for Gunther, so it is almost certainly his primary residence. I also contacted the owners of the building where the tavern operates, and they confirmed that their renter is none other than Oliver Gunther. I was hoping that I could find something wrong with his licensing or paperwork, but I verified that he runs the tavern legitimately. His liquor license, business license, and taxes—everything checked out. In other words, on the surface, Oliver Gunther looks like a philanthropist who also happens to run a bar.

"The report of Harrison being homeless reminded me of the first night I drove by to check out the Hemlock Tavern. I had seen a guy fitting his description, and he stuck out in my memory because he kept watching me, too. I went back Friday night to try to find him, and to confirm his identity. I walked around the building outside to no avail. But I eventually found him inside at a table. He played into my hands easily enough, and even gave me his name outright. But based on Moti's description, it's obvious that this drunk was not Kite himself. But I wanted to find out if he might know of Kite by name, and so I tested him. He went pale as a ghost, and I couldn't help laughing at my success. I don't have any evidence that Harrison is actually *involved* with Kite. But I at least know that he's *aware* of him. I also hoped to provoke this man Kite into some action. When Kite is told of me poking around, he might be tempted into a careless mistake, like sending Wilkes to try to bump me off. But I think he's smarter than that, so I'm just trying to get him to try *something* —*anything*! Our hands are tied until he makes a move!

"Now consider all of this, Jacobs, from the eyes of a defense attorney. We want to arrest a *police officer* because his hair was found inside a *police station*. And we want to arrest a *homeless drunk* because he was in a particular *tavern*. And we want to arrest a *philanthropist* whose good deeds help desperate women and children in the community. Every court in the world would view *us* as the villains!"

Jacobs' eyes puckered together, as he began to feel the dilemma. He looked down in thought, then back at Clarke, "As you said, we've got to catch him in the act, don't we?"

Clarke quietly shouted, "Yes! That is why I ordered Gunther to be under constant surveillance, and the men have been on him since yesterday. But this means catching him in the act of *killing*. And even if we win, it may be that someone else loses."

"And what about Wilkes?"

"I'm keeping tabs on him, as well. But my real concern is Moti. I assume that Harrison told Kite that I mentioned his name. And if Wilkes is working for Kite, then he might attempt to kill Moti ..." and Clarke seemed startled, and stared at Jacobs as he nearly whispered, "Darrell."

Jacobs asked confused, "Darrell? You mean that guy who hung himself in his cell a few months ago?"

Clarke was now picking up his things to rush out the door, and said, "It wasn't suicide, Jacobs. It was murder. Darrell knew about Kite, so *Wilkes* murdered him and made it look like suicide. *There's* our evidence. If we can find Wilkes' DNA on any of the evidence from Darrell's cell, we may have him!"

Jacobs remained sitting, and said, "Since you're obviously in a hurry, I guess I'll pay the bill. Dine-and-dash is against the law, you know. But one more question. Have you informed the Chief?"

"I am scheduled to meet with him this morning—but I need to get Darrell's evidence to the forensics lab first." And like a whirlwind in a library, he skipped around the tables and slow-moving servers, his turbulence blowing napkins to the floor as he heedlessly continued running toward his car.

Chapter Fifteen

Later that morning, Joseph was sitting on the edge of his bed still only semi-conscious, and delirious from sleep—or rather, lack of it. Although Lillian had remained at the hospital in the intensive care ward, Joseph continued to sleep in the spare room bed. The master bedroom had not been disturbed since the paramedics had hauled Lillian out of bed, and Joseph wasn't ready to see it just yet. His head slowly began to clear, and he hobbled to the kitchen to make some coffee and breakfast.

In his guilty state of mind, Joseph's conscience seemed to be hyperactively condemning him for every little thing he did, whether bad or not. For example, as he sat down to breakfast, he began to feel guilty for simply *eating*. He thought to himself, "Lillian is lying in a coma in I.C.U., and here I am enjoying *breakfast*!" And he began to feel like he was the worst human being ever created. But then his rationality asserted itself, "Well, if I don't eat, then I won't be able to do all that I need to do, whether for Lillian's sake or my own. So I refuse to feel guilty for satisfying my necessities!"

As he continued eating, he began to critically analyze his own conscience, as if it were a spreadsheet of data to be interpreted. But this time he wasn't trying to discover an anomaly in departmental spending. He was questioning, verifying, and testing his own mental and moral stability. For several weeks, he had justified the idea of murder to himself, and his conscience had been mute. How could this internal officer of right-and-wrong be so wrongly quiet about such wickedness as murder, and now so wrongly vocal about such pettiness as eating breakfast? If his own conscience was so unreliable, what about the conscience of others? Was the very notion of "right and wrong" somehow wrong itself? Or perhaps, was it just his own conscience that was off balance, while the rest of the world was healthy and whole?

As Joseph finished a bite of toast, he was taken back in thought to a time in his childhood when he was similarly biting a cookie. He soon got in trouble by his mother, and she scolded him for "ruining his appetite," and "not getting permission." This led his six-year-old mind to think of cookies as something that gets you in trouble. Yet the very next day, just after lunch, his mother freely gave him a small plate with two cookies and a glass of milk as a treat. He pondered this: the day before, his mother told him that eating a cookie was *wrong*, but today it was *right*. Of course, he didn't care about these quandaries at the time because the sugary delight of cookie-munching was a sufficient distraction. But what he could not possibly understand at that time began to become clear to him now. The source of knowing right from wrong was *moral authority*.

From his first memories, right and wrong had always been defined by his authorities: his parents at home, the teachers at school, the pastor at church, or the God of Creation. These authorities approved or disapproved of his behavior depending if it would help or hurt him, whether in the moment or throughout his life. These authorities were *moral* and *good*, so their approval meant he was doing *right*, and their disapproval meant he was doing *wrong*. And although this seemed dogmatic to his now-adult mind, he recognized this as the cause of his now-damaged conscience: he had become self-centered, self-important, self-governing, and self-assured. His conscience, so faulty and sick, was merely a symptom of the truth, that for many years he had disregarded any significant influence from moral authority. *He* had become his own authority. And now, sitting at the breakfast table, he could see how he had lost the security he felt as a child. It was not the loss of innocence or naivety that had destroyed his moral certainty, but his internal rebellion fueled by the pride of self-sufficiency.

Joseph's head shamefully bowed as he whispered, "God, help me."

The complete silence was suddenly disturbed as the refrigerator across the room made a quiet click and began humming. Joseph looked up, and happened to glance at the clock. It was already nine-thirty in the morning. He quickly cleared the table, then began making phone calls. He called Lillian's workplace, and Sarah answered. He explained that Lillian was in serious condition at the hospital, and would not be in to work today, and possibly—he chose his words carefully —possibly for the rest of the week. Sarah was audibly affected, and promised to communicate with all concerned. Joseph proceeded to call his own boss, as well as Charlie and Alan, and inform them of his situation. Then, with all of his childhood memories so freshly recounted, he decided to call his parents. He had always felt natural affection for his parents, but his inherent independence as a child, now fermented for two decades, had made him uncommunicative, to say the least. But something this morning had revived a need, a desire for their involvement. His mother answered, and after her repeated interjections of joy at his calling, he explained the grave situation as gently as possible.

He could hear her relaying the news to his father in the background, who then came to the phone, and simply said, "I'm so sorry to hear the news, son. Hang in there, and we'll do whatever we can to help you along."

After cordially thanking them, Joseph explained his urgent need to ready himself and be off to the hospital. He hung up the phone and began weeping again. He had almost expected them to chastise him for having not called in so long. He certainly hadn't expected them to show such love and concern. And in that five minute call, something unseen from their hearts and souls was transferred to his own.

As Joseph entered the I.C.U. ward, he saw Doctor Deiter happened to be walking his direction, but evidently hadn't recognized him. Joseph stepped in his way, and imposed himself, "Excuse me, Doctor?"

Doctor Deiter's eyes fixed on Joseph and seemed to be running his facial features through a database in his mind when he replied, "Ah, Mister Brighton."

Joseph could not conceal his nervousness, "Saturday evening, you mentioned that twenty-four hours were critical. It's been almost forty hours, and since my visit yesterday, I still haven't heard anything. How's she doing?"

The doctor graciously explained, "Well, Mister Brighton, I understand how you must feel, and I apologize if I have not updated you. The reason I have not reported anything is because there is very little to report. On Saturday, I honestly expected something to change within a day, but very little did. Her temperature has bounced around one degree lower. But she is still in critical condition, and has not regained consciousness. Again, I expect the next twenty-four hours to tip the scales. But aside from that, I assure you we're doing all we can. Please excuse me."

Joseph continued to Lillian's room, and sat on the edge of the chair beside her bed. He leaned forward so he could talk to her without being heard, and softly began, "Lily, I really wish you would wake up. There's so much I want to tell you—things you won't believe to be coming from me. I know the past few years have been rough, and I'm starting to realize that it's been *my* fault. I've become so evil—more than you know—and so selfish, I can understand why you've been so upset. I am so sorry for what I've been, and how I've treated you. But I promise to do better, if you'll just please wake up, and give me another chance."

Some physicians recommend that when a patient is comatose it can be helpful for family and friends to talk to them, play their favorite music, or share stories. Some people who have come out of comas have testified of varied degree of awareness, even quoting conversations that took place when they were seemingly unconscious. Medical research has proven the value of this, and a study of several comatose patients showed increased brain activity in MRI scans when recordings of loved ones were played.

Joseph paused and looked at Lillian, hoping that his words might have provoked some response. But she just lay there gaunt and frail, unchanged. Joseph stood up next to her bed, gently touching her hand. It was hot-to-the-touch, and this made him even more anxious. "Please don't die on me, Lily," he said in desperation. "Please come back, and let me make things right again, like when we were young."

Four hours had passed since Joseph had stood at Lillian's bedside, and the stress and waiting had caused him to drift to sleep in the chair beside her. Nurses were now bustling through the room, and the clatter caused Joseph to stir. He sat up squinting, and fearing the worst, he asked, "What's going on? Is everything okay?"

The nurse smiled, "We've good news, Mister Brighton. Your wife's fever broke less than an hour ago. We were just changing the bed linens, and making her more comfortable."

Joseph stood up, and could see Lillian beyond the nurse nearest him who was now slouching, and tucking in the clean sheets. Lillian was lying there looking frail, and her eyes were gently closed. The nasal cannula had already been removed, and she no longer had the unnatural look of being comatose, but simply looked like she was sleeping. Despite these improvements, Joseph was still eager to see her awake, and his concern was showing on his crumpled forehead. He glanced at the medical monitors beside her bed, looking for comfort, but in his troubled state, he looked away in revulsion. He looked back at Lillian's face, and was surprised and relieved to see her eyes were open, and connected to his own.

The nurses had finished their work, and were now rolling their large industrial laundry basket out the door. As the last of them exited the room, Joseph walked nearer the bed, never removing his eyes from Lillian. The solace imparted to him by her recovery could not conceal itself, and his features smoothed into a gentle grin that shone with sincerity. As Lillian looked up at him, her confusion could not conceal itself. She tried to speak once or twice, then managed to moisten her throat enough to ask, "What happened?"

Joseph looked at her as if she was a dried out flower that might lose a petal if he breathed too much or spoke too loudly, and answered softly, "You got sick, and fell into a coma. You've been unconscious for more than two days."

Lillian slightly scowled, mustered her strength, and retorted, "The nurses already told me that! I mean, what happened with *you*? You look different."

Joseph's head bowed humbly, "I hope I *am* different, Lily," and he looked up at her apologetically. "I'm *ashamed*, not just of what I've *done*, but for what I've *become*. But I have decided, no matter what happens, to try to be a better man, and a better husband. And I'm hoping that you will forgive me—for *everything*."

Tears were running from Lillian's eyes, down behind her ears, and she was subtly shaking her head as she responded, "No ..." But her words were cut short as her voice seemed to disappear into dryness.

Joseph was wounded, but asked, "No? Will you not forgive? Please, Lily, I admit that I've been horrible, but I really did hope that …"

As he spoke, Lillian was both shaking and nodding her head, while simultaneously waving her hand and pointing to the side.

Joseph was desperately perplexed, "What is it?"

As she emphatically pointed at a carafe and cup on the night stand, she managed to quietly croak out, "Water!"

Joseph promptly poured her a small cup of water and carefully handed it to her.

She quickly sipped, swallowed, and sighed. Her voice now revitalized, she continued, "I meant, no, the problem has not been *you*. The problem has been *me*." She began to cry, and spoke through her tears, "When you sent me those cucumbers, I realized that, if my father was still alive, he would be ashamed to have me for his daughter. And I was *glad* that he was not here to see what I have become. I am actually far worse than anything you have ever thought or said, and I am so sorry!" And she began sobbing.

Joseph reached out, and taking her hand in his own said, "I'm sorry, too, Lily. But it's going to be okay. We're going to work this out. It's going to be okay."

Chapter Sixteen

By Monday afternoon, it was evident that Lillian's health and strength were quickly improving. Her appetite had returned, and she had welcomed both the small brunch and late lunch offered her by the medical staff. Although the I.V. tube was removed, she was kept overnight in the hospital "for observation," as they told her. Joseph was certain she was feeling better when she insisted that she needed her purse, makeup, and fresh clothes before she could leave the room.

Joseph returned home, changed the master bed sheets, cleaned the room with rose-scented disinfectant, and tried to make things appear cared-for. For a moment, he reflected on how these unselfish acts yielded such personal satisfaction, and how much happier he felt when trying to make someone else happy. He spent the night at home, and slept for the last time in the spare room. But this night was different, and this lonely bed even felt more snug. He wasn't abandoning his rightful place in the master bedroom out of spite or feelings of rejection. Instead, he was attempting to preserve the neatness of the bed and the pristine cleanliness of the room so that Lillian would feel that special sensation of being the first one to use it. It was one of those generous acts that transforms commonplace things—such as cucumbers—into special symbols of unbreakable bonds. It was one of those intangible gifts that makes love more tangible.

Joseph returned to the hospital Tuesday morning with everything Lillian had requested, and after she spent nearly an hour getting ready, she emerged looking like herself, and eager to go home. The doctors recommended that she should try to stay off her feet for a few days so that her immune system could be restrengthened by rest, and Joseph assured them he would be staying home to help.

By Thursday morning, Lillian was feeling entirely stir-crazy. She had spent so much time in bed that she simply could not sleep another minute. Her body and mind forced her awake just before dawn, and every aspect of the room seemed to be fraught with irritation. In reality, the air was fresh, the sheets were comfortable, and the environment was peaceful. But in her exasperated mind, she felt like Poe's unfortunate protagonist, strapped to a plank in Toledo's dungeons, covered with rats, and the pendulous axe ever coming closer. Lillian tried to breathe, but the air seemed stale and thin. She repositioned herself in search of comfort, but even the incredibly soft microfiber sheets on her bed seemed laced with needles. She looked over at Joseph, sound asleep on the other side of the bed, half-expecting him to be gasping for air, or moaning in pain. But he lay there in tranquility, deeply and smoothly breathing, sleeping like a farmer the day after the harvest was completed. Desperate for some activity, she quietly grunted, threw off her blankets, and decided to get up and make breakfast.

Despite happily waking to the smell of bacon and eggs, Joseph tried to gently chastise Lillian for not resting. She gave him a cynical glare, handed him his breakfast, and simply said, "Eat." There's a catchphrase in the business world that says "less is more." And this was a perfect example of what that paradox really means. Lillian had only spoken a single word, but Joseph's mind somehow received the following communication: "Joseph, I'm not a baby. I know that I was sick, but I'm feeling better now. I got up, and decided to make us breakfast. So instead of making me angry by trying to coddle me, just take the food I've prepared, make yourself comfortable at the table, and enjoy your breakfast without provoking me any further."

Peace is usually only obtainable through compromise, so Joseph calmly acquiesced, and the morning remained pleasant.

Sometime around nine o'clock, Joanna called to check up on Lillian, and good-naturedly insisted, "After work, I'm going to drop off dinner for you and Joseph. I know you're going to protest. But I don't care if you are the boss in the office, you can't stop me after hours."

Lillian laughed, "Well, then I suppose I'll follow *your* orders! In fact, I'd love to have some company. It's been relaxing to be home, and Joseph has been pampering me so much I hardly recognize him. But I think I'm basically back to normal. In fact, I wouldn't mind going out for a bit in the next day or two."

"That's a great idea!" Joanna exclaimed, as if something was said other than what was said.

Lillian asked bewilderedly, "What is?"

"You, getting out for a bit. You and Joseph could come over to our house for dinner tomorrow night, and afterwards we can play games, and you can enjoy yourself! Besides," then she sing-song spoke, "I happen to know that tomorrow is your *birthday*!"

Lillian looked up as if there was a calendar on the ceiling, "Is it? What's today? Oh my gosh, it *is*! I completely forgot!"

"Well, what'dya think? We can get together at my house with you as the guest of honor."

"That sounds really nice, Joanna. But Joseph might feel a bit out of place."

"Then what about having him invite a couple of his own friends? That way we can all meet some new faces, as well. So?"

Lillian paused, then decidedly answered, "I like it! Give me a second to run it by Joe."

Joseph said the diversion might be fun, but was worried about Lillian becoming too fatigued if she left the house. Lillian said that she would be fatigued if she didn't get *out* of the house, and Joseph wisely assented.

"We're on!" Lillian proclaimed with joy. "Thanks, Joanna. Tomorrow is going to be the best Friday night I've had in a long time."

The past week had been very eventful. Joseph and Lillian had both experienced epiphanies of self-awareness, and even some rediscovery of the best in each other. Like a rowdy child demanding complete attention, the tension upon their mind, body, and soul had utterly possessed their consciousness. They had almost entirely forgotten about Kite, but he had not forgotten about them.

Kite was sitting in his office at home. It was just before noon, and G and T would be arriving any minute. Hemlock Tavern had been closed for less than a week, and Kite's regular income was going to be reduced for several weeks. His mind raced with imaginings about why he had closed it. He saw himself as an innocent victim of a tyrannical government. He was just a child, playing by himself in the schoolyard, enjoying the jungle gym and swings. Then, the bully government stepped in, and pushed him to the ground. He was frightened and angry, but stood up to fight back. But the bully held him at arms-length while he futilely swung back, unable to land a blow.

Suddenly, G and T banged open the door, and nonchalantly strutted in. Kite glared in disgust, and jumped to his feet, slamming his hands on the desk, "You come barging in here like two stupid bears! Knock first!!!"

G and T were actually startled by his outburst, and were secretly terrified of Kite even when he wasn't angry. But they both did their best to play it off, and G grunted, "Sss-cool."

"Sit down," Kite demanded, "because I've got work for you both, and I expect you to follow my instructions to the letter." They obeyed, and their bear-looks melted into sheepishness as they sat awaiting orders.

Kite sat down, and proceeded, "Let's get to brass tacks. As you're both aware, I was forced to temporarily close the Hemlock Tavern, and I'm currently looking for a new location. When we reopen, I want to upgrade the equipment, furniture, and inventory. And that is going to require some investment capital up front."

T interrupted, "Kite, we ain't got money, if *that's* what you mean."

Kite looked him in the eyes, and glared a thousand threats as he calmly said, "Until you grow a brain, I don't want to hear you speak again. Now shut your hole and listen!

"*I* am going to provide the investment capital for *myself*. All you have to do is follow my orders, and once the new tavern is opened, you'll have your regular jobs back."

Kite stood up, and began to slowly pace like a wartime general. Seeing him stand made them nervous in their seats, but they didn't move.

Kite continued, "Some weeks ago, I received a unique opportunity. I'm not going to go into all the details, but let's just say that this single job will provide sufficient funds for all of my plans in the near future. Your part in this job is simple: I need you two to pick up a couple, and bring them to me along with their vehicle."

G opened his mouth to speak, but Kite pointed at his face and said, "Shut up! Listen!" G sullenly closed his mouth, and Kite continued.

"I want you to go to their house tomorrow night—I'll send you the address beforehand. Hopefully, they'll be out enjoying their Friday night, then you can break in through the back, and wait in the darkness until they return. I will give you some mild pepper spray that will keep them distracted long enough for you to secure them both, hands and mouth. You must be quick. Be sure they cannot make noise, and prevent them from using their phones. If everything goes well, stay there until about eleven-thirty. Then take them into their garage, and with the garage door still shut, load them into their own car. You should then be able to drive away quietly, without being observed by any neighbors. And don't forget to close the garage door when you leave. Stupid mistakes like that always cause some nosey neighbor to call the cops, and ruin the best of plans. Bring them here, unload them the same way as usual, and lead them up to this room. I'll be waiting here to receive them, and I'll give your remaining orders then. If, by chance, they end up being at home, then you may have to subdue them home-invasion style. If something goes wrong, and they are able to call the cops, then abort the mission, and stay away from me for a few days."

He paused for a moment, and looked at them both, sitting there as quiet as kittens. "Now you may ask questions."

Either all questioned had been answered, or they were too intimidated to ask. They nodded their salutes to his orders, and headed out the door.

Kite sat down with a frightening leer, and said to himself, "Tomorrow is going to be the best Friday night I've had in a long time."

Chapter Seventeen

Thursday afternoon, Detective Clarke was not at his desk. He was outside of the entrance of the Forensics Biology lab, and was nearly yelling at the unfortunate lab technician, Alex.

Alex spoke with stoicism, "I'm sorry, Detective, but the only evidence from the Darrell suicide that was in storage was the pants that he used to hang himself."

Clarke's face reddened, "I already told you, he didn't hang himself! He was murdered!"

"I'm sorry, but the file says it was suicide. But as I was saying, we swabbed and vacuumed, and there were no hairs, fibers, or debris to be found."

"You weren't supposed to be looking for *debris*, you're supposed to be looking for DNA evidence!"

"I'm sorry, as I said, there was no contact DNA evidence other than that confirmed to be from the victim."

Clarke growled in disgust, and looked away as if trying to find an idea he'd misplaced on the wall.

Alex interrupted his thoughts, "I'm sorry, Detective. We did all we could with what we had. Will that be all?"

Clarke looked back at him, and sighed, "I'm sorry, Alex. I'm not angry with you. I'm disappointed, that's all. I was expecting to find something conclusive, and I suppose I expected too much. Thanks for your help, and try to forget my frustration today."

Alex unaffectedly replied, "Okay. No problem. Thank you." And he walked back through the security door into the laboratory.

Like a horse that has lost its rider, Clarke habitually started walking back to his stable—that is, his desk. What could he do now? His only hope of arresting Wilkes seemed to have dissolved before his eyes. And what about protecting Moti? Clarke stopped, and turned on his heels to check in on the monitoring room. He approached the steel door which had a small and narrow wire-enforced window on the top half, and peeked in to see who was on duty. Gary sat languidly looking at the security monitors until Clarke's movement in the window finally caught his attention. Clarke pointed down toward the door handle, and pleaded with his eyes to be let in. He wasn't actually cleared to enter the monitoring area, but Gary knew him well enough, and admitted him anyway.

Clarke diplomatically spoke, "How's it going Gary? Keeping busy?"

Gary's eyes were already back on the monitors, "Ah, you know how it is, Clarke. It never rains unless it pours."

Clarke scanned the monitors, "So how's our boy, Mister Martinez?"

Gary pointed up and to the right at one of the screens that was changing back and forth between two cameras, "He's as lively as ever, just sits there all day, watching T.V. mostly. I've been meaning to ask you about him. You said that he was a suicide risk, but I've seen him laughing out loud at T.V. shows, and once I even caught him crying during an old movie because the character's dog died. He seems pretty normal to me."

Clarke smiled assuringly, "Well, that's why I wanted him observed. He's clever enough to fool *you*, Gary. So we can't take enough precautions."

Gary was confused by this statement, and was trying to figure it out when Detective Clarke suddenly pointed at Moti's monitor and said, "Who's that?!?"

Gary hit a button which stopped the monitor from cycling, and fixed it displaying Moti's camera. Walking into the room was a man carrying a ladder in one hand and a toolbox in the other. He was dressed in blue jeans, and wore an industrial-style jacket, a work cap, a dust mask, and slightly shaded glasses.

Gary stared for a moment, and said, "I'm not sure. Let me check if there's any work scheduled in there today."

As he was reaching for the phone, and dialing the Facilities Maintenance Department, the man had quickly setup the ladder under the camera, climbed a couple rungs, and—pretending to clean the camera—obscured the view with a piece of cloth.

Gary continued to listen to the phone ringing, and said, "*That's* weird. Maybe we should get someone to check it out."

But his words were spoken only to himself. Clarke was already out the door in a flash, running to the detention area at a frantic pace. While he was running, he flagged down two armed officers by yelling, "Emergency! Follow me!"

Clarke hurriedly opened the security door, and the entourage burst into the area where Moti was being held. His cell door was open, and there was a struggle going on inside. The workman was standing over Moti, strangling him with a fragment cut from bedsheets. The armed officers drew their weapons and one of them shouted, "Stop! Don't move or we'll shoot!"

The workman put his hands in the air, and Clarke observed that he was wearing gloves. Moti still lay on the bed, gasping hysterically as he tore at the cloth around his neck, and coughed his way back to normal breathing.

The officers exchanged nods, and one of them walked up behind the workman. The officer removed handcuffs from a pouch attached to his belt behind his back. The workman remained motionless as the officer pulled each of his arms down, one by one, and cuffed him. They led the workman out of Moti's cell, and the officers were astonished by what Clarke already knew. When they removed the hat, the glasses, and the mask, there stood Officer Wilkes!

Clarke had the officers frisk Wilkes, but he was not carrying a gun. They did find his cellphone, which Clarke personally removed to prevent any warnings from being sent to Kite. Clarke also had his gloves carefully removed, and placed in plastic evidence bags.

Wilkes looked at Clarke with an Archaic smile, and said, "Well, Clarke. I guess it's been nice knowing you."

Clarke grinned back, "Yes, Wilkes. I suppose you meant that as some sort of a death threat. And I suppose you expect your buddy Kite will be the one to do the job. But only street scum and children use aliases to bolster their insecurities. So let's be clear. We're talking about *Oliver Gunther*, right?"

Wilkes jaw fell open, and his pupils contracted like a rabbit on a meadow road staring at approaching headlights. He was startled and frozen to hear that name from the lips of the smirking detective.

Clarke continued to gloat, "Yes, I'm quite aware of your ex-sergeant. And I'm fairly confident that he'll be joining you in here very soon. But that's not all I know, so let me just show you all of my cards. I know that *you* murdered Frank Darrell, right here in this very room, just over seven months ago. And I know that you were prying into Officer Jacobs' files last month, collecting details on Mister Martinez here. Then you sold that information to Gunther, who killed Ross Boyd that very night, and used the info you provided to frame Martinez. Gunther, no doubt, also planted the jewels in Martinez' van. And, if I remember right, wasn't it *you* who suggested we should search the van? I'll make sure you're also charged with conspiring to incriminate another. But in the light of everything else, I doubt that will matter much."

Then Clarke stopped smiling. He walked up close to Wilkes' face, and looking from eye-to-eye continued, "But you were quite wrong in what you said, Wilkes, at least from *my* perspective. It has *not* been nice knowing you. But it will be very nice to assist the prosecuting attorney at your trial, and to watch you be put away to rot. Yes, *that* will be very nice—from *my* perspective, of course. And if, by chance, we ever meet again in the free world, I suppose you'll be too old and decrepit to make good on any of your threats. So how about you just shut your trap, and exercise your right to remain silent."

Clarke took a step back, and motioned for the officers to take Wilkes away for booking. Moti had managed to sit up on the bed, but was still shaking and frantic. Clarke walked over, and put a comforting hand on

Moti's shoulder as he calmly said, "Mister Martinez, if you're quite recovered, please come with me, and I'll help you on your way. You're free to go."

Chapter Eighteen

"Come on, Joe! I don't want to be late!" Lillian prodded as she stood in the living room, leaning toward the bedroom. It was already six-thirty on Friday night, and nearly a week of feeling confined had made her excited to get out. She always enjoyed spending time with Joanna, even if it was just talking over lunch. But tonight, the novelties of meeting new people, sharing a homey dinner, and playing some games was something she had been looking forward to all day. She wasn't really interested in the celebration of her birthday, and even begged Joanna not to make much of it. She just wanted to *go*, like a sailor who's been out to sea for six month, and was finally approaching the home port. She had been ready to leave for almost an hour, as if applying her clothes and makeup would somehow speed up time. But contrariwise, every passing minute now seemed to drag on longer in her enthusiasm for the evening's recreation.

Joseph came out wearing slacks and a casual collared shirt. Lillian looked at him, and joked, "We're going to *dinner*, Joe, not to play *golf*.

He replied, "I know. That's why I wore sneakers."

She smiled and rolled her eyes as if to say, "Sometimes you're such a nerd," but walked out the door without a word.

When they arrived at Joanna's, everyone else was already there. Lillian looked at Joseph and raised her eyebrows as if to say, "I *told* you we were late," then cordially smiled and greeted the other guests. There was Joanna, her husband David, Sarah the receptionist, Joseph's friend Charlie, his wife Jan, and Joseph's friend Alan. Joseph and Lillian's arrival turned the room into human popcorn. Everyone stood up, shook each other's hands, exchanged names, and sometimes shook the same hand again. The air popped with, "Hello, I'm Alan." "I'm Sarah." "I'm Joanna's husband, David." "It's Jan, right?" "Nice to meet you." "You too." "Thank you." And after a minute, the popping people once again settled down into their seats.

Everyone thought the dinner was spectacular, which included a fresh spinach salad, fettuccini pasta with strips of grilled chicken seasoned with pesto, and toasted baguette slices topped with garlic, butter, and salt. Charlie was the first to say, "Mmm, this is delicious!" And thus he triggered an avalanche of praise from around the table: "Yes, Joanna, this is remarkable!" "The chicken is so juicy!" "What is this dressing? It's wonderful!" "This pasta tastes exotic!"

Joanna politely thanked everyone, and added, "David actually grilled the chicken. He's my master chef on the grill!"

When the dining was done and the table cleared, Joanna suggested that the game she had planned would best be played in the living room. Sarah sat to one side of the sofa, with Lillian in the middle, and Joseph to her right on the other side. Alan took the chair next to the sofa, near Sarah's side, and Charlie and Jan happily sat on the loveseat. David and Joanna brought in two dining chairs from the table, and made themselves comfortable on the side of the room opposite the sofa.

Lillian had been thoroughly enjoying the respite that this evening provided, and she now sat expectantly grinning like a child going to an ice cream shop. Joseph, too, was visibly pleased and sitting in anticipation. But like the trick whipping of a tablecloth, their joy was ripped from their faces and turned to shock when Joanna said, "The game we're going to play is called *Hitman*!"

The horror of that word struck to the heart of Lillian. She suddenly remembered her experience with that horrible man, Kite. The awful request she had made of him, and the terror that it might *still* happen. This brooding paralyzed her expression as she sat motionless on the sofa. Joseph's thoughts and reaction were much the same, though perhaps more introspective. He figured he must have subconsciously suppressed his memory of his own wickedness as some complex defensive mechanism. Or perhaps, as a moment of insanity, it was purged from his now-recovered consciousness. And several other theories about his memory lapse bounced around his mind as he sat there in a stupor.

Unbeknownst to both of them, there was an infinitesimal point in time when they shared the exact same thought: "I must find Kite immediately, and stop him from doing anything!"

Joanna broke in on their daze when she said, "Lillian? Are you feeling okay?"

Joseph was still lost in thought, but robotically turned to look at Lillian when he heard her name.

Lillian's head twitched slightly as she looked at Joanna, and tried to laugh it off, "What? Oh! Yes, I'm fine. Sorry. My mind was just wandering."

Joseph forced a chuckle, and tried to recompose himself.

Joanna's concern slowly waned, and she recovered her jovial mood as she explained the rules: "Okay, here's how the game is played. I'm going to start as the moderator. The moderator passes a card to each person, and whoever gets the ace-of-spades is the *Hitman*."

Joseph and Lillian subtly trembled.

Joanna continued, "All of us just continue to sit here and talk about whatever you want. But you have to continue looking around the room, and making eye-contact with *everyone*. Only the Hitman is allowed to wink with one eye. So if someone winks at you, then you've been 'hit.' After you've been hit, wait a few seconds, and then—this is the fun part—you 'die' as dramatically as possible. You can pretend that you were poisoned, shot, stabbed, or reenact your favorite death scene from a movie."

Other than Joseph and Lillian, most of them were laughing at the thought of dramatically dying.

Joanna concluded, "When you're looking around the room, try to catch the Hitman when they're winking at someone else. If you think you know who it is, then you can raise your hand and accuse them. If you're right, then you win. If you're wrong, then you're out of the round. Everyone understand?"

Sarah asked, "How does the Hitman kill you again?"

Alan interrupted, "He winks at you with one eye, like this," but his wink at Sarah was exaggeratedly flirtatious, and this made her blush, even though she was obviously flattered.

Joseph and Lillian clearly had difficulty enjoying the game. After a few rounds, when David was the current Hitman, he said, "Lillian, I've winked at you twice already, but I'm wondering, are you ever going to die?!?"

Everyone roared in laughter, and Lillian excused herself, "I'm sorry, David. I guess I'm still feeling a little weak from all the excitement."

At the end of the round, Joseph jumped on Lillian's queue, and said, "Well, Lillian's still in recovery mode, so I should probably get her home now." To his surprise, Lillian looked at him thankfully, as if he had correctly read her mind.

During the drive home, both were silent and pensive so that they hardly noticed one another. Lillian was rehearsing her plans in her mind, to return to the Hemlock Tavern—unaware that it was closed down—and how she feared to meet with Kite again. Joseph was trying to think of a way that he could drop Lillian at home, and go to the tavern this very night. But their relationship had just started to improve, and he was afraid of sending it once more into a downward spiral.

As they pulled into their driveway, Joseph pushed a remote control, and waited for the garage door to completely open before pulling inside and parking. He pushed the button again, and—brrrkt!—the low hum of the motor closed them in like a giant stone door to an ancient mausoleum.

Lillian was the first to enter the house, with Joseph immediately behind her. The house was entirely dark except for a dim nightlight that automatically turned on in the kitchen. And before Lillian was able to flip the light switch, an arm extended from the darkness and—sssst!—her eyes were burning, and she was coughing uncontrollably. Joseph had no time to understand what had happened before—sssst!—he too was hacking and debilitated. Joseph couldn't see anything, but he heard Lillian squeal for a moment, then her voice and coughs were muffled. A second later, someone was grabbing him, and used tape to cover his mouth, and bind his wrists and knees.

Joseph and Lillian were forcefully led into the kitchen, and made to sit down at their dining table. One of their assailants began to speak, and his voice sounded familiar to Joseph. He was certain it was G, the bouncer he met at the tavern. G was worse than a dentist apologizing for their pain, and said, "Don't worry, you two. That stuff is super-mild, but I'll grab some milk, and it'll help."

Joseph's fear began to turn to anger as he heard G speak like it was his own house they were in. G walked to the refrigerator, took out the milk, grabbed a cloth from the sink, and poured some milk on it. He washed their faces unceremoniously, and they were able to open their reddened eyes. G took a large chug of milk straight from the jug before walking back to the refrigerator, and callously replaced the container.

As Joseph glared at G, his thoughts began to sound like a misused customer who wanted to complain to the management: "What does G think he's doing? *I'm* the one who placed the order. They've obviously messed up for some reason, and maybe they think that *I* was supposed to be the *target*. Wait until I talk to Kite! I'm *certainly* not going to pay for this kind of horrible service! I have a mind to demand a refund!"

Lillian was actually feeling like she might faint. It had nothing to do with her recent sickness, as she had certainly made a full recovery. It was just a natural reaction to the fear of being overpowered, and the terror of what might happen next. She had never really paid attention to T's face the night he escorted her to Kite's, and she was so scared now that she failed to recognize him as the second thug in the room.

G and T waited according to Kite's orders, and at eleven-thirty, they walked—or rather hobbled—Joseph and Lillian back into the garage, and forced them into the back seat of their car. They placed black fabric hoods as blindfolds on them both, and searched Joseph's pockets for his keys. In a few minutes, they had quietly exited and closed the garage, and were safely on their way to Kite's house.

As they approached the house, T pulled out a second remote, and the garage door began to open. But as they paused while it opened, neither G nor T realized that at this very moment, they were being observed. Down the street, hidden in the shadows between the street lights, a black car with dark-tinted windows sat, occupied by two surveillance officers. One of them tightly held his night vision binoculars to his eyes, and relayed his observations. "Two in the front, and two in the back wearing hoods—looks like they've taken hostages."

"I'm calling it in," the other urgently replied, and picked up the radio.

Joseph and Lillian, with their legs secured by tape just above the knees, were nearly dragged along through the house, and led into Kite's meeting room. They were still blindfolded, but each of them were sure they knew where they were. The protocol was somewhat different this time, however, as they were both forced to sit down, and then tied to their respective chairs. G and T then left the room, and closed the door behind them.

Sitting blind, mute, and restrained, Lillian was whimpering through the tape, and sniffling in trepidation. Joseph, still convinced that he would sort out this obvious misunderstanding, sat fuming with anger.

Kite had been sitting at his desk, watching these two before him, when he was suddenly overcome with amusement. He snickered at first, followed by a chuckle, which swelled into a few giggles, which built into open laughter, then burst into bellowing belly laughs. Ordinarily, laughter can be a contagion as people will often laugh at someone else who is laughing. But there were greedy and degenerate tones in Kite's hilarity that were more appalling than appealing.

He winced as he restrained his mirth, and simultaneously pulling the hoods from off their heads, he announced, "Welcome, Mister and Missus Brighton!" And he once again burst into merriment.

He carelessly pulled the tape off Lillian's face, and she immediately screamed as loud as possible. The scream obviously irritated Kite's ears, and the levity left his face. But he unaffectedly walked toward Joseph, saying, "Go ahead and scream. Five or ten more screams like that and you won't even be able to speak. Besides, I've had this room soundproofed, and no one else can hear you." And he ripped the tape from Joseph's mouth.

Joseph growled in pain, but quickly tried to address the current situation. "Mister Kite, there's been a misunderstanding."

Lillian looked at Joseph revolted, "You know him?!?"

Joseph glanced at her, and ignoring her question proceeded to speak to Kite, "Also, I've changed my mind. I don't want you to do anything after all. So just let us go, and we'll be on our way."

Lillian's mouth was wide open as she looked back and forth between Joseph and Kite, like a spectator at a tennis match.

Kite had sat down at his desk, folded his hands, and smiled at Joseph. Then he sneered at Lillian, and asked, "Do *you* have anything to say?"

Lillian was still stuck looking back and forth, and then asked Kite, "How do you know Joseph?"

Kite laughed again, and arrogantly said, "You should both remember that I'm in the business of knowing people. So let me tell you what I know, and then I'll tell you what my plans are for this evening."

Kite stood, and began militantly pacing so as to deliver his monologue momentously. "About a month ago, Mister Brighton here came to request my services in regards to his wife. During our interview, what wondrous coincidence should happen? Missus Brighton was in this very house at the very same moment, also wanting my services in regards to her husband."

Joseph scowled at Lillian, "You mean *you* know him, too?!?"

Kite proceeded, "As you are aware, I tend to know *everything*, and I was able to quickly learn that both of you together are worth over a million dollars! My humble services are a mere two percent of that amount. Of course, since I had already gotten the first ten thousand out of you, Mister Brighton, it was only *one* percent at the time. And I realized that I couldn't very well make satisfied customers of you *both*, otherwise, I wouldn't get any more from either of you! So I figured out a way that I could take care of you both, *and* enjoy the things that you would no longer need."

Lillian grimaced at Joseph, "You gave him ten thousand dollars?!?"

Joseph wouldn't look at her, but gently replied, "No! Well, not directly. I just made a donation to his charity. It *is* tax deductible, after all!"

Kite paused, walked over to his desk, and took a document contains five stapled pages out of the drawer. Tauntingly holding and shaking it, "Do you know what this is, Mister Brighton?"

Joseph glared, "No, but I'm sure you can't wait to tell me."

"It your wife's will."

Lillian blushed, and looked away. Joseph's glare turned at her.

Kite gloated, "I convinced Missus Brighton here that she could get a special deal. Instead of paying me fifty percent up front, she could 'temporarily' write her will over to me. Then once the job was done, she could pay me the full amount at once, and change her will back. Mister Brighton, you really did marry one of the dumb ones, didn't you? But that doesn't matter now because I'm going to do what *both* of you asked me to do! I've decided to stage a little accident. You, Mister Brighton, are going to 'fall asleep at the wheel,' and drive you and your wife off a cliff. And, if your car doesn't start burning on it's own, I'll give it a little *spark* to get it going. Once you're burned up car is discovered charred on the rocks, all of your money and assets will be distributed to me by your ever-so-faithful lawyers!"

Joseph looked at Lillian, "So, are you going to tell him?"

Lillian's eyes scowled back, "Joe! Shush!!!"

"What do you mean, 'Shush'! This guy's going to *kill* us because he thinks he's going to get our money!"

"Joseph Brighton, stop talking! You're going to make him mad!!!"

"Mad?!? He's already mad! He's as crazy as pet coon under a full moon!!! But if he's going to kill us for our money, he should at least know that the will he's holding is *useless*!"

"Joseph! Stop!!!"

Kite had been trying to listen to this exchange with patience, but now demanded, "Wait! What do you mean this will is *useless*?"

Joseph looked at Lillian, "Tell him!"

Kite growled, "No! I've had enough of you two bickering!!! You, Mister Brighton, will explain—now!"

Joseph couldn't help looking defiantly, as he began, "It all goes back to when we were kids …"

Kite interrupted, "Stop!!! I don't care about your life story! Just tell me about this will!!!"

Joseph retorted, "It's useless because of our prenuptial agreement."

"Why?!?"

"Because our prenup was written so that it intentionally overrides any *independent* will that we may create. In short, unless we *both* execute a will together, our prenuptial agreement overrides everything, and makes the will void. Lily, you know this!"

Lily blurted defensively, "Of course I know this! Do you think I'm so stupid that I would bequeath everything to a complete *stranger*? Especially someone like *this* guy?!? I figured that if he …" She began crying, "if he actually killed you, then I'd just pay him in cash, and then the fake will wouldn't matter. But, Joe, I'm so sorry! I'm ashamed of everything I've done! These past few days have been refreshing, and I want you to know …" She sobbed out the words, "I love you!"

Joseph was deeply moved, and tears ran down his cheeks. "I love you, too, Lily. I'm so sorry! It's *my* fault that we're here!"

"No, my darling! It's *my* fault!"

Kite had walked around the desk, and pulled out a small pistol from the top drawer. Realizing that he had been played like a fool, he was nearly grinding his teeth, and his jawbone cut through his thin skin displaying his anger. He stepped in front of Lillian, and—click, click! —cocked his gun. All was silence.

Kite looked fiercely at Lillian, and pointed the gun at her head. He shouted, "You little whore! You think you can mock *me* and live?!? I don't usually kill for free, but you two are more than I can take!"

Lillian stared down the barrel, and began trembling in shock.

Joseph protested, "Wait! Don't shoot her!!! Let her go, and kill *me* instead!"

Kite paused, sadistically savoring the panic on Lillian's face, and the quivering of her breathing. "Alright, Mister Brighton. You first."

The next few seconds seemed to pass in slow motion. Kite was turning to aim the gun at Joseph, and stepping that direction at the same time. Lillian was twitching, and still staring into the space where the pistol had just been. That same instant, the door behind Joseph's back burst open, and an armed policeman jumped in. It was Officer Jacobs. He quickly saw the gun in Kite's hand and shouted, "Stop!" as he took aim. Kite was startled by the intrusion, and in reflex—bang!—he pulled the trigger, and Joseph fell limp in the ropes binding him to the chair. Lillian began screaming in horror, then fainted. Jacobs opened fire, and Kite flew backwards across the room, banged into the wall, then slid down into a motionless pile. Jacobs called out for assistance, and kept a bead on Kite as he slowly walked over to him. Two more officers piled into the room, and quickly began examining Joseph.

Kite lay bewildered and gasping, but managed to turn his head toward Jacobs and say, "That really hurts." Then his head fell sideways, and he hissed out his last breath.

The other officers had cut Joseph's ropes, and laid him stretched out on the ground. They were now kneeling over his body, energetically compressing and trying to bandage the area on his shoulder now stained with blood. Lillian was reviving but still stupefied as Jacobs stood behind her, working to cut her ropes, and calmly reassuring her that the danger had past.

Chapter Nineteen

Beebeep, tick-tock, beebeep, tick-tock. Joseph began to awake to the sounds of a heart monitor, and an industrial clock. Opening his eyes seemed as difficult as if they had been sewn shut, and the best he could presently manage had him peering through the web of his own eyelashes. His mind seemed to be standing on top of a wall between the reality he could see and the reality of subconscious thought, and uncertain which side was an illusion. He lay there looking out from his dreamworld for several minutes, trying to grab ahold of his consciousness. But like a greased pig, it kept managing to slip his grip, and run around squealing and mocking. Eventually, the devious little porcine clown seemed to stand still, and Joseph was able to capture his wits.

Near the right side of the foot of his bed were Doctor Deiter and Lillian. The doctor spoke quietly as Lillian stood with one arm hugging herself, and other raised with her hand gently and anxiously pinching her bottom lip. Joseph remained motionless, and listened.

"Your husband was fortunate that the bullet missed the subclavian artery, or he would not have survived. He did, however, suffer some muscle damage to his right trapezius and platysma, as well as a chipped clavicle. The surgeon was able to remove the bone fragments, and the clavicle itself should be fine in about six weeks.

Bones are remarkable self-healers. In short, your husband should make a full recovery."

Lillian sighed, "That's good news, doctor. Do you know when he'll wake up?"

"The anesthesia should be worn off by now, so …"

Joseph rasped, "I'm here."

The doctor smiled, "Like I said! I'll leave you two alone."

As he walked out, Lillian drew near the bed. Her eyes were teary, and her countenance was oppressed with anxiety, shame, concern, and lack of sleep. Joseph's eyes were now half-open, and he glanced up weakly grinning, "You look terrible."

She laughed with tears and sniffled, "You should see *yourself*!"

"What happened? I don't remember anything after …"

"Right when you were shot, the police burst in."

"Did they arrest Kite?"

Lillian shook her head, and closed her eyes as if to erase a memory.

Joseph asked, "Was he …?"

Lillian cried and nodded, "Shot? Yes."

"Dead?"

She nodded again.

Joseph closed his eyes feeling a mix of relief and shame. "What happened to us, Lily?"

She grabbed his right hand with her own, and combed his hair with her left hand, "I've been thinking about that all night, Joe. When we were young, I was able to see the *best* in you. I wasn't blind to your faults, but I was happy to overlook them. Then something changed. I started to *search* for faults, and *ignore* your goodness. I don't know why I became like that." And she wept.

Joseph looked up as he squeezed her hand lovingly. "I did exactly the same thing, and I think I know why. It was that cursed prenuptial agreement! We became so obsessed with following the *letter* of the law that we failed to follow the *spirit* of it. At the start, that agreement was a symbol of our love and commitment to one another. But when we failed to maintain the *spirit* of that love, and we become filled with pride in ourselves, and hatred for each other."

Lillian looked at Joseph as if he had shone a flashlight into a darkened room, and exposed the filth and clutter. "I think I see," she said.

"We've got to destroy it, Lily," Joseph continued. "We've got to stop building our marriage upon it, and get back to the simple love that brought us together in the first place."

Lillian burst out weeping in joy, like a prisoner held in a dark dungeon when the doors are suddenly opened and they are declared to be free. She fell on Joseph, and kissed his lips with a passion not unlike their wedding day. She squeezed and hugged him, not noticing his grunts of physical pain until at last he cried out audibly, "Aagh!"

She jumped back, "Oh! I'm so sorry! Are you alright?" She continued weeping, "I just feel like this burden was lifted off of me, and I feel like I can be *myself* again." She whimpered joyfully, "I feel *love* again!"

Joseph smiled through his discomfort, and reached out for her hand. His tone revealed his heartfelt sincerity as he said, "I am very much in love with you, Lily, and I want this to be a new beginning," as he tenderly smiled. He reassuringly continued, "I'm sorry I groaned so loud a minute ago. My shoulder and neck are quite sore, and it really was involuntary."

She smiled, gently leaned over, and kissed his forehead. She continued standing by the bed, as they both admiringly held and stroked each others hands.

Three weeks later, the trials for the remaining members of Kite's gang began.

Harrison had been arrested for questioning, but was of little use in obtaining any information at all. During interrogations, he seemed to fall back on his military training, and would only repeat his name and service number. There was ample evidence to prove that he had been a sort of resident at the Hemlock Tavern, and that he had a loose affiliation with Kite. But there was no tangible evidence that he had any knowledge of Kite's crimes, nor did Harrison offer any confessions. In the end, he had to be released, but was required to be present at all of the coming trials. They told him that this was "in case you're called on to testify," but in reality, it was so they could get their hands on him quickly if any evidence against him came to light.

G and T—whose real names were revealed to be George Tucker and Antonio Marson respectively—were both tried for multiple crimes including accomplice to first-degree murder, kidnapping, and several other lesser crimes which the prosecutors included just for good measure. They were both convicted of the major counts, which carried mandatory sentences of life in prison.

The Wilkes' trial became one of the most highly publicized trials of the decade. Because of Wilkes' position on the police force, Moti's wrongful imprisonment, the attempted murder when Moti was in jail, and the dramatic nature of Kite's criminal ring, the trial was daily reported and became commonly known among the public. Some news commentators expected Wilkes would receive the death penalty, and some went as far as to suggest that he should.

During the trial, Kite's phone records proved that Wilkes had been commissioned to kill both Frank Darrell and Martin Martinez. And Alex, the forensic technician, was required to testify how an analysis of Wilkes' personal gloves—the ones he was wearing when he attacked Martinez—also contained contact DNA from Frank Darrell. Wilkes' attorneys desperately attempted an insanity defense. But the truth was, despite Wilkes' criminal activities, he had an excellent record on the police force, and had always passed his psychological reviews. The jury unanimously found him guilty, and he was sentenced to life without the possibility of parole.

Moti had been summoned to testify at two of the three trials. But his testimony was more of a technical procedure than a practical one. All he was asked to confirm was that George Tucker, also known as G, was the man who took him to Kite's, and that he recognized Wilkes as the man who had tried to strangle him. But there ended up being some lasting good that came from him being there.

Because of the media interest surrounding Wilkes' trial, as both Moti and Harrison were exiting the courtroom, they were quickly surrounded by prodding reporters, cameras, and microphones. One reporter asked Harrison a string of questions, "Did you know Kite? Is it true you live on the streets? What are your plans now?"

Harrison sadly looked up, "Well, I'm hoping to get a job, and just try to live a normal life."

Moti looked at him, and felt a sense of pity and compassion. With all the cameras of the world watching and listening, Moti blurted out, "You can help me clean carpets, if you want."

Harrison's eyes teared up, "Are you sure? I don't know how."

"It's easy," Moti assured him, "and I can teach you all I know!"

They both shook hands, and there was a spontaneous applause from the people surrounding them.

When the owner of a local auto dealership saw Moti's charity on the news, he was moved to show some charity in return—as well as foster some good publicity. He called the news station, and arranged for Moti to come down to the dealership where he would receive a brand new van, outfitted for cleaning carpets. The exposure Moti gained from these videos being repeatedly broadcast on television caused his business to boom. Within six months he had grown to a fleet of three vans, employed four "specialists," and Harrison—now clean, shaved, and free from alcohol—was his bonafide business partner.

"Now," Moti thought to himself, "all I need to do is find a good woman who will be my wife!" And he felt sure his search would end in success.

Throughout the trials of Kite's gang, Joseph and Lillian not only attended several of the proceedings, but they also felt compelled to closely follow all of the news. Although it was distasteful, and even traumatic for them to relive, they wanted to know that they would be free of reprisals, whether criminal or legal. When they heard the sentencing of G and T, it certainly helped to settle their minds on the one side. And on the day of Wilkes' sentencing, as they were leaving the court, Detective Clarke pulled them aside. He seemed to be aware of their anxiety, and assured them with a warm yet suggestive grin that *all* cases were now closed. They nervously thanked him for the information, and finally felt that they could move on with their lives.

But the headlines also brought to their attention something that wrenched their hearts. One of the reporters had discovered the three shelters that Oliver Gunther had operated, which currently housed over one hundred suffering women and their children. Due to his death, these shelters were now at risk of being shut down, which meant that these already suffering families would be forced out. As Joseph and Lillian talked this over, they began to consider if they might be able to interfere for good. They stepped forward, and made their proposal to the banks. With their joined cash and assets as collateral, they were able to obtain loans, to purchase all three of the shelters, and to continue the operation of those bittersweet communities. The high-profile nature of their kindness attracted many donations, some of which hailed from enormous national corporations. And in just over a year, all of the loans for the shelters were able to be paid off, and there was a steady flow of charitable donations and funding sufficient for the foreseeable future.

Three years later, on a beautiful and warm Sunday afternoon, Joseph and Lillian returned home from church. Joseph parked the car, and both he and Lillian quickly jumped out and opened the vehicle's back doors. Lillian unbuckled their grinning and chattering two-year-old from his car seat as Joseph was unstrapping the carrier that contained their little girl, a five-month-old bundle of joy. They had discovered that only by working together could they have new lives.

Epilogue by Detective Clarke

As an investigator, I have learned that sometimes the most important and persuasive evidence is invisible to the eye. I don't necessarily mean that it is microscopic. I mean that many people see things everyday, and either overlook their significance or fail to connect their importance to the case at hand. And the present "case" for each of us is, of course, our *life*.

The Brightons had fallen into this mistake. Although, as they later told me, their relationship began with all the makings of love and joy, they had lost their ability to *see*. They had become effectively blind to their need for one another, and arrogantly believed that they were somehow enlightened. But pride is always present when there is darkness and contention in the heart, just like humility associates itself with light and love. It is actually this theme of darkness and light, and black and white—in a moral sense, of course—that I want to discuss.

In my youth, I tended to see people as either good or bad. Good people lived their lives in peace, and contributed to society without making designs or inflicting harm upon others. Bad people did the opposite. Good people earned their right to be free citizens, and bad people forfeit their rights and freedom. This ideology seemed to serve me well as an enforcer of the law, and later as a detective of crime. But I think

I have since learned better, and wanted to share my discoveries.

I no longer believe that people are simply good or bad, or "black and white," as I previously described. Within that metaphor, I would say that people are more like shades of gray. There is no one who is purely good, and there is no one who is purely bad. That is to say that sometimes people who are generally conscientious or "good," as you may call them, can fall into moments of weakness or darkness. A *light* person might have vices that make them a *shade of gray*, if you will. Likewise, even some of the most sinister people I have encountered—Oliver Gunther, for example—can also have a positive effect on society, and their *absence* can seemingly cause more suffering than their *presence*. They seem to be a *dark* person, yet with virtues that also make them a *shade of gray*—however dark that shade may be. And the most difficult reality that I have observed is that *everyone*, no matter how "good" they think themselves, is capable of falling into intense darkness. In other words, we are, all of us, complicated heroes and complex villains.

Please do not think that I am implying myself as a judge over society. Indeed, I see myself as a mere observer, and a member of the greater whole. My point is not to cast judgment, but rather to prevent it. And this is where I feel myself in need of grace, and compelled to willingly and humbly confess my reasons for saying so.

During the Kite ordeal, after Wilkes was arrested, I initially felt like I had atoned for the death of Frank Darrell. I had caught his murderer, and finally justice would be served. But when I remembered that Darrell was wrongfully arrested in the first place, I realized that it was *I* who put him in that cage and made him vulnerable to his assailant. Naturally, I objectively rationalized my actions, that based on all I knew at the time, there was nothing else I could've done. But I began to see that, as I served *justice*, however noble and right my intentions, I sometimes caused collateral damage that was *unjust*. I still believed deeply in the *rule of law*, and that justice was a necessity of society. But how could I reconcile the suffering that I had caused through my passion for justice? And now I will tell you my conclusions.

By definition, justice must be *just*. This means that justice must be *right*—or more accurately, *righteous*. In other words, the act of serving justice must be founded on a principle of protecting goodness, not merely on the principle of punishing badness. Besides, as I already said, *all* of us have *badness* sometimes, and if punishment was perfectly administered for every infraction of the law, we would *all* be behind bars! Therefore, I decided that as a detective, I could no longer try to punish every offense of the *letter of the law*, but I would certainly not hesitate to enforce the violations of its *spirit*. And I interpreted the *Spirit of the Law* as being the need to protect the public from wickedness in society, and to punish those who created or supported that wickedness. In essence, the law was intended as *protection* first, and *punishment* second. And now, I'm afraid I will test what sort of person *you* are—whether judgmental or redemptive—as I offer the following confession.

Obviously, I knew that Moti had originally approached Kite in a drunken rage, and seeking revenge. And when I reviewed the logs of Kite's text messages, I discovered that the Brightons had also approached him for his services—separately, of course—the very same day that I had visited them in their home, no less! As the detective on the case, the prosecuting attorneys were dependent upon me to provide them with evidence. And now I confess that I never presented the evidence against Moti or the Brightons to anyone, nor did I reveal it to my trusted comrade, Officer Jacobs. In my estimation, Moti was not a killer, but a victim. And when I later observed Mister and Missus Brighton, their mutual love and respect was so evident that I destroyed the evidence against them. That's right. *I*, a detective of crime and an agent of the law, violated the law. And I did it for the sake of *protecting* people who could be redeemed, and might otherwise have been condemned. And I feel justified by the ancient truth, that "the letter kills, but the spirit gives life." And now, I am dedicated to that truth.

One more thing, if you don't mind me asking for a favor, please treat this information as confidential. It might be better for all of us if the Chief of Police didn't read it.

Signed,

—Detective William Clarke

Other titles you may enjoy, available in both print and e-book formats:

Freedom To Choose
By E. L. Kidwell
ISBN: 978-0-9817634-1-5
Visit the Kingdom of Heaven before Earth was created. Enter the throne room of God, and experience the events before time began. Discover the secrets of why hell's chief accuser betrayed the love and perfection of His Creator, and set himself to destroy the race of mankind in seething hatred. Enjoy this thought-provoking drama as it brings to life the Genesis account of the Bible.

The Pilgrim's Progress
Part I and Part II including
detailed Table of Contents
By John Bunyan
ISBN: 978-0-9817634-3-9
This timeless class of John Bunyan "delivered under the similitude of a dream" captures the hearts and minds of readers with Bunyan's depth of understanding and scriptural knowledge, as well as his subtle comedy and witticisms. This edition contains both parts of Bunyan's tale, including all of the original scripture references in an easy-to-read format, as well as a detailed Table of Contents to easily jump to favorite events in the story.

www.ingramcontent.com/pod-product-compliance
Lightning Source LLC
Chambersburg PA
CBHW031336170626
46807CB00002B/717